TOO MANY COOKS

A BARTLETT AND BOASE MYSTERY

Who would imagine a little gold ring could lead to kidnap, torture and even murder? How could the curse of the Pharaohs come to Falmouth? The year is 1923 and a young Cockney woman appears in Falmouth. Inspector George Bartlett and Constable Archibald Boase thinks she's harmless enough – until she and they are caught up in a seemingly endless cycle of mayhem and deceit. When a strange visitor claims to be a relative of the tragically-murdered Russian royal family, Bartlett and Boase have little time left to prevent further murders as their superintendent looms large in the background waiting to take them off the case...

TOO MANY COOKS

A BARTLETT AND BOASE MYSTERY

by

Marina Pascoe

Magna Large Print Books
Long Preston, North Yorkshire,
BD23 4ND, England.

British Library Cataloguing in Publication Data.

Pascoe, Marina
Too many cooks – a Bartlett and House mystery

A catalogue record of this book is
available from the British Library

ISBN 978-0-7505-4229-6

First published in Great Britain in 2014 by Accent Press Limited

Cover illustration by arrangement with Accent Press Ltd.

Published in Large Print 2016 by arrangement with
Accent Press Limited

Magna Large Print is an imprint of Library Magna Books Ltd.

Printed and bound in Great Britain by
T.J. (International) Ltd., Cornwall, PL28 8RW

For Kevin, Erin, and Olivia

With love and thanks

Chapter One

Desmond Cook, a fine-looking young man of twenty-four, never let the sun burn his face, although he regularly stripped off his clothes and donned khaki-coloured shorts and a sleeveless vest in the sun to make sure his body was as brown as could be. A friend of his, having lived in Egypt for several years, had warned him that sun on the face was dangerous and, if it didn't kill you, you'd end up looking old before your time. Desmond, a man who attracted all the local girls of Falmouth, had no desire to become old before his time. The very expression conjured up images of the weather-beaten fishermen he had seen mending their nets or landing the day's catch, their skin parched by the wind and sun. So, handsome Desmond Cook, with his black, wavy hair, green eyes, and slim six-foot frame so popular with the ladies, was going to keep his youthful looks for as long as he possibly could.

Through the last three long, hot Cornish summers, Desmond was regularly seen lying in the sun in Falmouth's sub-tropical Kimberley Park. Although no one ever saw his face, which was always covered with a jumper or jacket – anything at all would do – the locals strolling through the park, and all the children playing there, knew it was him. Several would say as they went by, 'Afternoon,

Desmond,' and were never offended when no reply came – the sun made him sleepy. His parents said it was time he got a job; since he had come down from Oxford in 1921, he had done nothing but have fun. He was well-educated and lazy. He lived, mostly, with his parents in a very smart house on Florence Terrace. He also owned a small flat – he wanted to be independent and his parents didn't always approve of his lifestyle, particularly when he wanted to stay out late and return in the early hours. His father, Dr Mortimer Cook, gave him a very substantial allowance but, four weeks ago, had threatened to withdraw it if Desmond didn't find work by the time 1923 was over. Now, in early August, with the sun shining again, Desmond would worry about all that later – even if he didn't start looking until mid-September, something would turn up. For now, he settled down with a heavy calico tunic covering his head – he didn't want to fry his brain, after all; he'd need that to get a decent job and to stop his nagging father. So, on that hot Saturday afternoon, legs, arms, and chest exposed, Desmond Cook basked in the heat of the sun, listening to the birds, to the children screaming as they chased each other around the park, and to the few people who uttered, 'Afternoon, Desmond.'

It was no surprise at about ten o'clock the next morning, with the sun's rays already too uncomfortable for most, when those leaving St Mary's Roman Catholic Church and enjoying the park on their way home saw Desmond yet again, in his usual spot in the corner, in his usual pose – horizontal.

David Nankivell, who had been working on the park's flower beds the day before with his father, Harry, had got into trouble when he returned home; he had left his father's best trowel in one of the beds.

'I told you not to touch my tools,' his father had said, 'you've got a perfectly good set yerself. You'd better go back for it.'

'But, Da, it's dark now an' I can't remember where I put it – I won't be able to see a thing. I promise I'll go in the morning. No one'll 'ave bin in the park overnight anyway, yer trowel'll still be there.'

'Hmmmmm, it'd better be,' came the reply.

So it was on the Sunday, David Nankivell was searching in the beds for his father's precious trowel. He looked up as he heard dainty shoes clicking on the path behind him.

''Ello, David, workin' on a Sunday?'

It was Iris Hellings. A pretty young girl of nineteen, the same age as David, the two had met on their first day at the National School in 1910. Iris had always liked David and the two had remained friends even after they both left school. Now, the funny little girl with plaits and freckles had become tall and elegant and the mousy hair was a lovely shade of gold. David got to his feet.

'Hello, Iris, what're you doin' 'ere?'

'I'm just off to meet Mary – we're goin' for a walk along the sea front.'

Iris and Mary Butler both worked in shops in Killigrew Street, Iris in the post office and Mary in a baker's shop. They walked to work together, went to dances together, styled each other's hair – everything, the two were inseparable.

'Wish I was goin' with you – I've come back to look for Da's trowel an' it's not 'ere – 'e's goin' to go mad. I thought I left it over there,' he said pointing to a raised bed about fifteen feet away, 'but I couldn't 'ave.'

Iris felt sorry for David and she watched as he ran his now dusty fingers through his short blond hair and saw the beads of sweat that began to trickle down his forehead and onto his red cheeks.

'Shall I 'elp you look for this trowel, then?' she offered.

'Won't you be late for Mary?'

'No, I'm a bit too early anyway – come on, two pairs of eyes are better than one, we're bound to find it if we both look.'

'Thanks, Iris, that's really nice of you.'

The two began to search under every bush and in every bed. After about fifteen minutes they met up. David was looking worried.

'Any luck, Iris?'

'No, I'm sorry, David, nothing. 'Ave you thought about asking 'im?' She was pointing across the park to where Desmond Cook was stretched out on the grass.

'What, Desmond? 'E won't 'ave seen anything – all 'e ever does is lie there like a starfish.'

'Let's ask 'im anyway, it can't do any 'arm.'

David and Iris made their way across the park towards Desmond. As they drew nearer, David called out,

'Desmond, oi, Desmond – you 'aven't seen a trowel round 'ere 'ave you?'

No reply came and David turned back towards Iris. ''E's asleep as usual, I don't want to disturb 'im.'

'Well, I do.'

Iris ran past David and as she reached the spot where Desmond Cook lay she let out such a scream that David thought the whole of Falmouth must have heard it. He crossed the grass to where she stood and looked down as she pointed. From beneath the calico coat covering Desmond in the usual way, blood trickled and had formed a pool on the path next to where he lay.

David didn't touch the coat but called out again, 'Desmond, Desmond – are you all right? DESMOND!'

'Of course 'e's not all right – 'e's dead.' Iris began to shake. David grabbed her arms.

'Iris, behave yerself – go across to Dr Chalmers's 'ouse – that one over there with the blue door – get 'im to come – quick!'

Iris ran across the park, out through the green gates and crossed Kimberley Park Road. She saw the blue door; it was a blur, she couldn't think straight now. She ran as fast as she could through the doctor's garden gate, tripped up the steps and reaching the door, hammered on it for all she was worth.

'Help, help, somebody, please, please come, Dr Chalmers!!'

She continued banging on the front door until her hands were sore. After what seemed to Iris an absolute age, the door opened and there stood Dr Chalmers, an old man with white hair and a ridiculously large white moustache. He was dressed in a quilted gown and wore slippers.

'What on earth is going on here, young woman? It's Sunday morning and I'll thank you…'

'Oh, please come, please ... in the park ... I think 'e's dead.'

Dr Chalmers could see by the look on her face that Iris was in a complete state of panic.

'Wait here, my dear, I'll fetch my bag.'

Within seconds the two were hurrying down the road and heading for the park, Dr Chalmers still in his gown and slippers. They went in through the park gates and hurried to where David was standing. Dr Chalmers, seeing the amount of blood told David, 'Get that young woman out of here – run as fast as you can to the police station, take her with you. Fetch Inspector Bartlett – if he's not there get that young Boase. Don't delay!'

David grabbed Iris by the hand and together they ran back out onto Kimberley Park Road and towards the Falmouth police station which was situated about a quarter of a mile away.

In the park, Dr Chalmers knelt down on the ground beside Desmond Cook. Blood stained the bottom of his green quilted gown, turning the silk to black. Fearing the worst on account of the volume of blood on the ground, the doctor slowly lifted Desmond's coat and reluctantly peered underneath. He dropped it back down quickly, his suspicions becoming horribly true. Desmond's head wasn't there. No one seeing him from a distance would have known – why, wasn't this how Desmond always lay in the park during the summer months? Dr Chalmers, despite having served for many years in the army as a doctor and having seen some appalling injuries in times of conflict, was shaking. He'd only once seen anything like this and it was something he'd hoped never to see again. He waited beside poor Desmond's body and hoped Inspector Bartlett would be quick.

Reaching the police station and very much out of breath, David and Iris burst through the front door. The desk sergeant stopped them.

'Just a minute, you two, where's the fire?'

'Please, sir,' David took a deep breath, 'please, sir, we need Inspector Bartlett – or Constable Boase; it's very urgent, sir.'

'I'm sure it is, young man, I'm sure it is. But, Inspector Bartlett is a very busy man, as is Constable Boase – sure I can't 'elp you?'

David was becoming irritated at the delay.

Iris stepped forward, her composure somewhat regained now.

'Please, Dr Chalmers says Inspector Bartlett, or Constable Boase, must go immediately to Kimberley Park – something serious 'as 'appened – 'e said for Inspector Bartlett to be quick.'

The sergeant looked at Iris's tear-stained face.

'Just you wait 'ere a minute – I think they're both in this morning, although I confess I don't know why they bother on a Sunday.'

Within a couple of minutes the two policemen appeared from their office. George Bartlett, the tired, cynical older man, weary from a life of hard work, and his young assistant, Archie Boase, eager and with a sharp mind which Bartlett admired.

Bartlett had moved some years earlier from his job in London where he had been working as a detective; his wife was unwell and he had thought the sea air would be good for her. He had to go back to uniform and take a reduced salary but it was worth it to see his wife's health improving. His superior, Superintendent Bertram Greet, was a hard man to please and neither liked the other. Greet, however, saw Bartlett as an asset to the station and gave him, usually, free rein, assisted by Boase. Greet didn't like to see them in uniform – he felt it made people nervous so he usually insisted that the two men appeared in mufti whenever they could. They were normally investigating something important and it suited Bartlett to wear his own comfortable clothes – he never did like uniform, he maintained that it made him feel like a servant.

The two men were at the station this particular morning because Bartlett had been woken by hammering on his front door at half past five; he had opened it to a young man, Eric Tresize, a youth known to Bartlett as his father, Arnold, often competed against Bartlett in the county flower shows. Eric had been walking up Penmere Hill in the direction of Bartlett's house on his way to work as an apprentice at the Falmouth docks when he had seen a man climbing out of the front window of the house at the end of Bartlett's terrace. Eric saw the man walk calmly around the side of the house and disappear. By the time Bartlett had run to the house, the man had gone. Eric thought this must be the Trawlerman, a burglar who had been operating in the town for almost six months, breaking into houses in the early hours or late at night and stealing jewellery. He was known as the Trawlerman ever since Bartlett and Boase had tracked down his haul on a small trawler moored on the river at Penryn. That had been about four months ago – all the jewellery had been successfully returned to its owners but the Trawlerman had escaped capture. Bartlett had called for Boase and asked him to come to work for the morning so that they could rethink their plans – the Trawlerman had not done any work for three weeks and the two detectives had hoped he'd left the area or given up for good. The event witnessed by Eric Tresize now seemed to indicate otherwise and Bartlett wasn't going to rest until he was caught. He was angry with himself for delegating the job to junior officers; they'd had no luck so Bartlett and Boase would have to find him. Now they were being interrupted again.

Summoned by the desk sergeant, the older man came out of his office and approached the two youngsters.

'Now then, what's all this about?'

David spoke hurriedly.

'Please, Inspector Bartlett, sir, Dr Chalmers says you're to come at once – something's 'appened in the park an' 'e needs yer 'elp.'

'Well, *what's* happened?' Bartlett relit his pipe.

'I don't know, sir, but there's a man – Desmond Cook – lying on the ground, bleeding.'

Iris intervened.

''E looks dead.'

Bartlett turned to his assistant.

'Come on Boase, let's see what this is all about – get a car; my knees are jiggered this morning. You youngsters go home, you've done a good job this morning – thank you both.'

David and Iris looked at each other. Iris was crying again.

'Do ... do you think 'e's dead, David?'

'Well, there was an awful lot of blood. Inspector Bartlett'll sort it out – you go off an' meet Mary, you're late now.'

'I don't think I feel like it now, not after such a shock.'

'She'll be waiting, Iris. Go on, go an' tell 'er what's 'appened.'

'S'pose you're right – thanks David. I 'ope you don't get into trouble about yer Da's trowel.'

David squeezed her hand.

'Doesn't seem very important now, does it? What about poor ol' Desmond – 'e's got a bit more to worry about. I'll come back later maybe. Da'll understand.'

The two parted company, David back to his home in Wellington Terrace and Iris to meet Mary at the Prince of Wales Pier.

A couple of minutes later Bartlett and Boase were drawing up outside Kimberley Park. Boase stepped from the driver's side.

'You don't think they were 'avin' a laugh, do you, sir? I can't see anyone.'

Before he could answer, Bartlett looked across the park and saw Dr Chalmers kneeling on the ground.

'Quick, Boase, Chalmers is over there, look.'

The two men ran across to where the doctor

was waiting, Boase's younger legs getting him there more quickly than Bartlett's. He knelt down and spoke to the doctor.

'What's 'appened, Dr Chalmers?'

The old man looked at Boase as Bartlett came towards them.

'Well,' he said, a tear in his eye, 'you can rule out suicide. I hoped never to see anything like this again at my time of life – there's nothing I can do for this poor young man.'

Dr Chalmers slowly stood up and looked at the two policemen.

'It's a youngster named Desmond Cook – I know his father, a very fine doctor. He and his wife are going to be devastated by this news. The poor fellow's been decapitated – oh! Who could do such a thing?'

Boase, at this news had turned ghostly white; he stood up from his kneeling position and turned away from the body.

Bartlett patted Dr Chalmers on the shoulder.

'Thank you very much, Doctor. I'm sorry you had to come out to this. Can I just ask you, sir, how long you think he's been here?'

'Well, maybe seven hours – a little more perhaps. You'll need a full examination of course.'

'Thank you, Doctor – you go on home now, you're not dressed to be out.'

Dr Chalmers had quite forgotten his attire. He picked up his bag and slowly made his way back across the park.

Bartlett turned to Boase. 'You all right, my boy?'

Boase was very shaken.

'I'm OK thanks, sir. It's just ... I saw things like

this in the war – I don't want to see it again.'

Bartlett was sympathetic. He wondered what his poor son, John, must have witnessed in 1916, in the days leading up to his own death on the Somme. He grabbed Boase's sleeve.

'Look, I'll wait here – you go and make arrangements for a full and thorough search of this scene and for the removal of this chap's body – but first, get rid of that rabble over there. Don't worry about this – we can't help the boy now.'

Boase thanked his superior and headed to the fence where about a dozen people had gathered, some pointing and chattering, others just staring. On seeing Boase coming towards them, most of the small crowd dispersed. Two young men loitered.

'Come on, you two – if you don't move along now, I'll take you in.'

They both left at top speed.

Shortly afterwards, Bartlett and Boase met up again at the police station. It was just after midday. Boase was already installed in their shared office when Bartlett arrived.

'Cuppa, sir?'

'I could do with one, lad – what a day we're having, and a Sunday too.' Bartlett was pleased to see that Boase's colour had returned and he looked much better. 'You all right now, Boase?'

'Yes, thank you, sir. Dunno what came over me this morning in the park – I just...'

'Save it, my boy, you don't need to explain to me. Right, Dr Chalmers said he would guess roughly that the body had been there for about seven or eight hours – that makes the time of the murder around two or three-ish. Boase, I want you to call in every police officer we can get to conduct questioning and then I want a re-examination of the area – I know the men are searching now but I want it gone over twice, three times ... we can't afford to miss anything and I really don't want Greet bearing down on me again, he's already been on the telephone asking questions that are impossible to answer. Can you organise that?'

'Straight away, sir.'

Anything serious like this and Greet would only give Bartlett three days before he called in detectives from London; that was really the last thing Bartlett wanted ... young, eager men coming in to the station at Falmouth, lording it over everyone ... no, Bartlett would nip this in the bud before there was a sniff of any outside interference. *But how?*

Boase went to co-ordinate the officers and Bartlett quickly finished his tea. A murder really was the last thing he needed at the moment.

Within twenty minutes every available officer was scouring the park and making enquiries of every house – particularly those overlooking the park and the spot where the body was found. No one seemed to be able to offer any information but the operation soon facilitated the spread of gossip around the town and news of the find went about quickly. Bartlett and Boase made separate enquiries and met up at about three o'clock. Bartlett's knees were aching.

'I thought all this leg work was over for me, Boase – and not a thing to show for it. You?'

'Nothing, sir. I suppose it was quite early for a

Sunday. I really hoped someone could tell us something – we've not got a single clue.'

'What about the churchgoers at St Mary's?'

'Someone's on that now, sir.'

'Something's not right, Boase – Dr Chalmers reckons that Cook was murdered at about three this morning?'

'Right, sir.'

'So, the boy was known to sunbathe in that spot regularly, even Dr Chalmers told us that ... but then why would he already be there the night before? That's preparation gone mad ... no, it's ridiculous – it doesn't make sense, does it? And he was wearing semi-formals.'

'Fair point, sir. Someone did tell me this morning that Desmond usually turned up at around ten, it was a Mrs...' Boase flipped through his notebook '...Mrs Chinn. She also said that he always wore shorts as far as she could remember.'

Bartlett was turning things over in his mind, why would Desmond Cook be up and in the park so early – well, in the middle of the night?

As the two men stood and Bartlett lit his pipe, Constable Ernest Penhaligon came running up to them.

'Sir, sir, we've just found this in the hedge – it's a glove; it's covered in blood, sir.'

He handed the item to Bartlett. The two men stared at the glove and then at each other.

'What do you make of this, Boase?'

'Well, it's definitely a woman's, sir – about a seven and a half, I'd say.'

'When did you learn so much about women's clothing, my boy? I'd say you're right anyway.

Thanks, Penhaligon, carry on.'

Bartlett looked again at the glove.

'Why would a woman's glove be here covered in blood, Boase?'

'The murderer is a woman, sir? Maybe an accomplice?'

'I don't know, Boase. No idea, but ... maybe it's a start.'

The two men and an army of police officers continued to search. At about half past six, Bartlett met up with Boase. The older man, warm and red from the heat of the August evening sun, sat on a wall and mopped his face with a large handkerchief.

'Now, we've spent nearly all day here – how about you come to our house for dinner tonight? Mrs Bartlett said she'd cook tonight instead of earlier on when I told her I didn't know what time I'd be back. Now, how about it?'

Boase hesitated – he had told his landlady he'd be back this evening.

'Irene's looking forward to seeing you again – it must be nearly two weeks since you two last got together.'

Bartlett knew which strings to pull with Boase – at the moment there was only one and that string had Irene Bartlett's name firmly on the end of it.

'I'd love to, sir, thank you very much – if you're sure Mrs Bartlett won't mind?'

'Mind? Of course she won't mind. She always looks forward to seeing you and you'd think she was cooking for ten most days, so there'll be plenty of food. Come over at, say, eight? I'll leave instructions for any more information to come straight to my house this evening – I've got every available man out in Falmouth tonight, whoever did this won't find it easy leaving the town.'

'Right you are, sir, good, that'll be very nice, thank you. It'll give me plenty of time to tell Mrs Curgenven that I won't be eating with her this evening.'

Mrs Thomasine Curgenven, Boase's landlady, was a widow of some forty years, having lost her husband in the very early days of their marriage. Boase didn't know why or what had happened – he wouldn't dream of asking. Now in her late sixties, Mrs Curgenven was pleased to have Boase's company in the big old house in Melvill Road. He had replied to an advertisement for a lodger in the *Falmouth Packet* when he returned from the war. He took to Mrs Curgenven immediately and she to him – she didn't need the money but, company, yes, and a policeman, well, better still. The two respected each other and got on very well. She had no children but one nephew who visited her about four times a year. Boase got on well with Michael Curgenven. The two had discovered on Michael's last visit that they shared a birthday, but Michael was older by three years. He was a successful chef with his own restaurant in Truro. He had told Boase, 'Archie, I really like you and I'm glad you're keeping Aunt Tommy company. Next time you're in Truro don't forget to drop in to the Delta and I'll be sure to give you a dinner on the house – bring a young lady if you like, I'll treat you both.'

Archie liked this idea – perhaps he could take

Irene. He'd heard all about the Delta, what a first-class restaurant it was with excellent food. Yes, he'd take Irene there one day – one day soon.

At a quarter to eight, Boase was turning into Penmere Hill and heading in the direction of the Bartlett house. He soon walked up the front path and knocked on the door. Immediately he heard a booming bark from the other side of the glass and he smiled. Topper was on guard duty as usual. Bartlett opened the door and on recognising Boase Topper, the Airedale terrier belonging to the inspector, squeezed past his master and jumped up on his hind legs to greet his guest.

'Topper, down, boy, let Boase get in will you?'

''Ello Topper, good boy, good boy.'

Boase pushed his way past the over-enthusiastic creature and followed Bartlett into the parlour. On a small table next to Bartlett's favourite armchair stood two bottles of Leonard's London Beer. The man from London's East End would drink nothing but this good old English favourite, still brewed today not more than two hundred yards from where Bartlett had been born almost sixty years ago. Bartlett held one of the bottles out to Boase.

'Here you are my boy – nothing but the best. Cheers!'

'Thanks, sir. Is Irene in?'

'Yes, she's in the kitchen with her mother – they'll be in presently. I went in just now to get some glasses and they threw me out. Don't know what they're up to.'

The two men didn't have to wait long to find out. Caroline and Irene entered the dining room

Caroline called through to the parlour.

'Dinner's ready you two, come on now.'

Bartlett and Boase didn't need asking twice – nor Topper. The three trooped into the dining room and waited to be directed to their places. Irene pointed to the chair next to hers.

'Hello, Archie. It's lovely to see you again. I've put you here, next to me – is that all right?'

'Yes, thank you, Irene.' Boase thought it was more than all right. 'How have you been keeping?'

'I've been very well, thank you, Archie – it seems like ages since I last saw you.'

To Boase it seemed more than ages. Irene looked beautiful in a cream cotton sundress with green polka dots and around her throat she wore a bottle-green velvet choker. Her hair was tied loosely in a bun and fastened at the back with a large green enamel comb. As always, she wore the golden bracelet which Archie had given her the first time he spent Christmas with the Bartletts in 1921.

The pair were very much in love but no engagement had been announced. Instead, they met maybe once or twice a week for outings or Boase had dinner at the house. Caroline, having been unwell for many years, was worried that Irene was not allowing the relationship to progress so that she could continue to live at home and help around the house – she had spoken to Bartlett about this and he was beginning to share the same concerns. But he had said, 'Well, Caroline, you know how stubborn our daughter is – just like her mother. If she wants to be with Boase, and I for one won't object at all, then she'll tell us soon enough. Just let the youngsters get on with it.'

So, for now, that was how it would be but Caroline was unhappy that her daughter was apparently sacrificing her own happiness for the sake of her parents.

Within minutes the four were sitting round the table and enjoying roast beef with Yorkshire puddings and vegetables. Bartlett and Boase wasted no time in emptying their plates.

'Irene's made us a very nice dessert, Archie, something with strawberries in,' said Caroline getting up to clear the table. 'Will you go and fetch it, dear?'

'Of course, Mum. You'll be impressed with Dad's strawberries, Archie, they're delicious.'

Boase stood up as Irene did. His action was immediately followed by a yelp from Topper who, unknown to Boase, had been lying under his chair and had now been stepped on.

'Oh! Topper. Oh, I'm so sorry, boy. I wouldn't 'urt you for the world. Let me 'ave a look. Was it your paw? Now then, let's see.'

Bartlett laughed.

'That dog always sits under *my* chair – are you switching your allegiance, Topper?'

Topper licked his master's hand reassuringly while Boase sat back down and stole a piece of fat from one of the plates for him.

''Ere you are boy, this'll make you feel better.' The dog took it eagerly.

'Archie, you're such a fool with that dog –

you're worse than Dad.' Irene was laughing but she was quietly pleased at how gentle and understanding Boase could be. Topper went to lay on the rug and Boase stood up once more.

'Can I help you with the pudding, Irene?'

'All right, thanks, Archie.'

The pair went together into the kitchen and soon the giggling and laughter began. Bartlett looked at his wife and smiled.

'Those youngsters get on very nicely together don't they, princess?'

'I've always said so,' replied his wife. 'Yes, I told you Irene could do much worse – I think they're very well suited, very well indeed.' Bartlett left the conversation at this. He wasn't one to get involved in affairs of the heart. His daughter was old enough and sensible enough to make her own decisions when it came to things like that.

After dinner, the four sat in the parlour, the two men now on their third Leonard's London.

'What about this business in the park today, Boase? And this Trawlerman, too. I think tomorrow we'd better rethink our plans – we could well do without a serious crime at the moment.'

'What happened today, Dad?' enquired Irene.

'You don't need to bother yourself about that, my girl – not a very pleasant incident, that's all you need to know for the time being. Now, the Trawlerman, well, that's another thing. I thought he'd gone away but seems I was wrong. He was spotted in this very road early this morning trying to burgle once more. Would you believe the brass neck of him?'

Boase nodded, Leonard's London Beer, a large meal, and a hectic day making him feel rather tired all of a sudden.

'I suppose we've got more important things to worry about now though, sir.'

'You're right, my boy, you're right.'

The clock in the hall struck eleven and Boase stood up.

'Time for me to go – I don't know where the time's gone,' he exclaimed looking at Irene.

'I'll see you out, Archie. It was nice of you to come.'

'Early start tomorrow, Boase, you look like you could do with some sleep.'

'Right-o, sir. See you in the morning. Thanks for a lovely evening, Mrs Bartlett.'

'You're more than welcome, Archie,' Caroline replied.

Irene walked Boase to the front door and the two stood on the step looking out onto the small front garden.

'Well, goodnight, Irene. Thanks for the lovely supper.'

'You're very welcome, Archie – will you come again soon?'

'I'd love to.'

The two stood looking at each other. Irene stood on her tiptoes and kissed him on the lips. He drew her closer and lost himself in the scent of lilacs in her hair. All too soon it came to an end. Boase didn't want to outstay his welcome and so he kissed her cheek and walked to the gate. He looked back and waved. Irene blew him a kiss.

Chapter Two

Bartlett and Boase were already in their office by seven o'clock the next morning. Constable Penhaligon had brought them a large pot of tea which was beginning to do the trick – Boase, not a drinker, was feeling the effects of Leonard's London Beer this morning and the hot, sweet tea soon worked its magic. Before long he felt almost human again.

'Strong beer that Leonard's, sir.'

Bartlett looked up from his work and peered over his reading spectacles, his brow furrowed in wonderment.

'*Strong? Leonard's?* Come on, Boase, what sort of a man are you? I can see you need to be better educated. Perhaps you'll join us at the weekend, I'll soon get you used to my London beer – best there is, you know.'

The weekend? Boase was thoughtful. Any kind of beer in any quantity was worth it if he could see Irene. Yes, he'd soon get used to Bartlett's beer all right.

'Right, Boase, finish your tea, I want you to come with me to see Dr Mortimer Cook. He's no doubt going to be in a bad way but we need to ask him some questions. I know it's early but I want to catch him before he opens his surgery, although I wouldn't blame him if he doesn't bother today – or ever again for that matter.'

Boase emptied his cup and the two men drove to the doctor's house on Florence Terrace.

The terrace was a row of very large, fine houses with verandas which gave out on to cottage style gardens. Bartlett and Boase walked up the path to the front door of number one, Bartlett knocked and the two men waited. Neither man knew Dr Cook well as they were both patients of Dr Chalmers. Boase observed the garden. A small, brown and gold sign in the shape of a hand with a pointing index finger read *SURGERY,* and was situated at about eye level, indicating the route for patients to take. A pleasant route it looked too; a narrow path, lined with many sorts of roses, which Bartlett had already espied and was giving a professional eye, and which led round to the side of the large house. Presently, the door opened and a tall man, seemingly in his mid-fifties, stood there. He had a trim white moustache and masses of thick, white hair. He was slim and wore a dark suit with a pale blue silk waistcoat from which hung a gold watch chain. He looked at the two men enquiringly but didn't speak. Bartlett recognised the man as Dr Cook, lifted his hat, and introduced himself and Boase.

'I need to talk to you, sir, about your son.'

The man graciously opened the door wide and motioned for the two men to enter. They found themselves in a large hall which was finely furnished with antiques including several Egyptian artefacts one of which, a large gold statue of a cat-like creature, stared at Boase with a gloomy expression in its eyes but a rather unnerving smile on its lips. The man led the way across the hall and into a large drawing room. More Egyptian relics there.

'Won't you please sit down, gentlemen?'

Bartlett and Boase sat on a rather large and soft day bed under a window. Dr Cook stood by the fireplace. Bartlett cleared his throat.

'We're very sorry about what happened yesterday, sir,' he began, 'I can't tell you what a regretful situation this is...'

'My wife will never get over this, Inspector Bartlett, this is all too much for her.'

'I'm sure it must be, Dr Cook, and I can assure you we'll do everything we can to find out who did this terrible, terrible thing. In the meantime, I'd like to ask you about Desmond, about his friends, what he'd been doing lately – was there anyone you could think of who would want to hurt him?'

'I can't think of anyone at all; Desmond was very popular, he had plenty of ladies chasing him, he had a couple of chums from his student days who visited occasionally – nice fellows, in good jobs too, one a solicitor and the other a private tutor – not like Desmond. He was a lazy young man, I have to say, Inspector Bartlett, but we idolised him, that is, my wife and I, and, of course, his cousin, Donald.'

'Could you tell me the names of these friends, Dr Cook?'

'Well, let me see, there's Charlie Wentworth – he's the solicitor, lives in Oxford. He's doing quite well, I believe. His parents live there and he's actually working for his father's firm. He was going to come down here for a short holiday in a week or two with the other fellow – a rather eccentric character, goes by the name of Leon Romanov. He swears he's related to the murdered Russian royals – who's to know? He lives in West London and teaches Russian to English students.'

'And what of your nephew, Dr Cook?'

'Donald? Donald's away at the moment, in Egypt. My wife and I looked after him when my brother Magnus was in the army and my sister-in-law was suffering very badly with her nerves; sometimes she could cope with Donald and sometimes it was just too much for her, consequently he probably spent more time here with us than with his own parents – but we didn't mind; he'd been coming to us since he was six years old. The boys became more like brothers. When Magnus contracted malaria and died we assumed total responsibility really. Sadly, my sister-in-law was killed in a motor accident shortly afterwards. Both boys had promising futures but I've had such a job getting them to do anything useful since they came down from Oxford – to be fair, Donald has only just finished, although he's spent every spare moment in Egypt; not his subject though, they've both been studying law but neither really seemed keen to pursue it as a career. I had always hoped that at least one of them would become a doctor like my brother and me but they didn't have any interest in it. It's always tomorrow. Donald has promised me faithfully that he'll find work when he returns from his travelling. He's gone mad on anything to do with Egypt ever since those fellows Carter and Carnarvon. He's been there a few times. I actually knew Lord Carnarvon, many years ago, and Donald had always been fascinated with the things he and Carter were getting up to in Egypt – even as a youngster. Carnarvon just died, sadly, a few months ago; Donald tells me the talk in Cairo is of a curse relating to a tomb – of course, I don't believe that, the chap caught something and died, simply that. You can see some of the souvenirs Donald returned with; he's practically filled the house with them. My wife said she would have been quite content with a bracelet – just a trinket, but, no, Donald had to bring back almost the entire contents of a tomb, I should think. I dread to think what he'll return with this time. I expect him back in about a fortnight. I haven't tried to get word to him about Desmond – I'd rather get him back and tell him myself, you understand. Of course, my wife and I miss him terribly, particularly now.'

Bartlett stood up.

'Well, you're a busy man, we won't keep you further, Dr Cook – do you have these two men's addresses to hand? We'll just check to see if they can help us at all.'

'Yes, I think I have, somewhere. Wait a minute please. I must be quick, my patients will be arriving soon, I can't let them down.'

'Quite. I understand.'

Dr Cook left the room. Bartlett looked at Boase.

'Very brave man. Bearing up better than I should.'

'Perhaps he's not all he seems, sir,' came the younger man's reply.

'That's a very strange thing to say, Boase.' Bartlett never disregarded his assistant's theories. This young man had a good brain and had earned

Bartlett's respect on many occasions.

'I just think, sir, it's too early to discount anything.'

'Yes, you're probably right, Boase. I just feel incredibly sorry for this family right now.'

Dr Cook returned. He handed a small leather-bound book to Bartlett.

'I hope this helps, Inspector – it's Desmond's old address book – I'm not sure how up to date it is – Wentworth and Romanov are in there – some others too, mainly women, I think. Desmond was a bit of a ladies' man.' At this, Dr Cook broke down and sobbed uncontrollably.

'He had everything to live for, he was clever, handsome, vivacious. I can't believe this has happened. I'll never get over this, never.'

Bartlett patted the doctor on the arm.

'I'm so very sorry, Doctor. If there's anything I can do, please let me know.'

'Thank you, that's very kind of you, but I must start work now. It'll help if I do something. I have to be strong for Ingrid. She's devastated.'

'I understand, sir. I'll let you know of any developments – and thank you for the address book. I shall return it as soon as I can. Goodbye, Dr Cook. We'll see ourselves out.'

Bartlett and Boase crossed the hall, walked back through the front door and towards the garden gate. A young woman dragging a small child was hurrying towards the surgery, the child was crying and trying to keep a bloodstained, makeshift bandage tightly around his hand. Bartlett lifted his hat as she passed and looked at Boase.

'That man Cook is going to find all this very

hard, Boase, very hard indeed.'

On returning to the police station, Bartlett and Boase were met at the door by Constable Penhaligon. As he delayed them at the entrance, Boase was looking through the pane of glass in the door. Inside, seated on a bench was a young woman of about twenty-five. She had red curly hair, on top of which she wore a small brown hat. Boase observed that the girl was wearing men's trousers under her long brown coat. He thought it strange, not just that the girl was wearing what appeared to be men's clothes, but that her clothes were more suited to winter than this hot August day. Penhaligon was speaking urgently to Bartlett now.

'You see, sir, she was actually in the park at that *very* spot – that's why we brought her in. I've been trying to get hold of you and Constable Boase but I didn't know where you had gone. We even found the other one in her pocket.'

'Thanks, Penhaligon – you've done all the right things. Go and put the kettle on, would you?'

Bartlett turned to Boase.

'Wait here on the step a moment, Boase. Did you hear what Penhaligon was saying? He reckons they found this girl rummaging for all she was worth in the bushes in the park in the same place that the glove was found – and she had the other one in her pocket. We'll have to talk to her, Boase.'

Shortly, the young girl was sitting in the inner office with the two policemen. She was clearly looking confused.

'Would you like a cup of tea, Miss?' Boase asked.

'Yes, ta, that would be very nice.'

Boase walked to the door.

'Penhaligon, make that three cups, would you?'

'Would you mind telling us your name, miss?' Bartlett was removing his coat and searching for his pipe.

'Me name is Sheila Parsons.'

'And where are you from, Miss Parsons?' quizzed Bartlett, recognising the pronounced Cockney accent.

'Well, I live 'ere in Falmouth at the moment, temporary like ... someone told me there was a situation for a maid but when I came down 'ere for the job I found out it was given to someone else – bleedin' cheek if you ask me. Before that I was livin' in Bethnal Green; I think I'll 'ave to go back there now – it's in London.'

'Yes, I know,' Bartlett was puffing on his pipe, 'that's just the area I grew up in.'

'No ... well, I never did, there's a thing. Innit a small world?' The girl relaxed immediately.

'Do you know if Mallinson's is still there? When I was a boy...'

The conversation was cut short by a loud cough from Boase.

'Yes, well, anyway, Miss Parsons, we'll have to talk about London another time, perhaps.'

'Oooh, that'd be luvly.'

'In the meantime,' Bartlett continued, 'can you tell me why one of my constables picked you up this morning in Kimberley Park?'

'Oh, that's easy – I lost something an' I'd gone back for another look, see?'

'And what exactly were you looking for?'

'Me glove, of course. Look, 'ere's the other one.'

She pulled the glove matching the one in Bartlett's desk from her pocket. There was no doubt – this was the other one all right.

'Could you tell us when you lost the other glove, Miss Parsons?' asked Boase handing her a cup of tea.'

'Yes, I lost it Saturday – ta ever so.'

'And why were you in the park?' asked Bartlett, cup in one hand, pipe in the other.

Miss Parsons paused to sip her tea.

'Well, it's me neighbour's cat, innit? When the maid's job was given to the other girl, I went a bit berserk – I told the mistress of the 'ouse that I'd just come all the way from London and didn't even 'ave anywhere to stay the night. So she said I could spend the one night – she was sorry for all the mix-up but I could 'ave the small room in the attic since it was getting late – very gracious, I'm sure. There's another girl wot works there – ever so nice she is, 'er name's Dolly, well, Dorothy I suppose, but "call me Dolly" she says. She said it was nice to 'ave someone 'er own age around an' as long as I didn't say nothin' to the missus, she wouldn't tell if I wanted to stay a couple of days more ... secret like. So I did. Anyway, where was I? Oh, yes, next to that 'ouse lives an' old lady – with Mr Hargreaves...'

'Mr Hargreaves?'

'Yes – the cat.'

'The *cat's* called Mr Hargreaves?'

Bartlett was leaning forward in his chair, making sure he had heard correctly.

'Yeah, that's right. 'E's a luvly, big, soft old thing. Anyway, I was goin' out this particular morning, Saturday, when the old lady called to me from the window. "Excuse me, Miss," she said, "please can you 'elp?" Well, always bein' one to do a good turn where I can, cos it don't ever 'urt to be neighbourly now – does it? Hmmm?'

Sheila Parsons waited for an answer.

'No, no, Miss – it don't ever 'urt,' replied Bartlett. Boase grinned at the older man's accent.

Sheila Parsons continued.

'So, I went up the path and there in the 'all was Mr Hargreaves' lyin' on the floor, sort of moanin' like. I picked 'im up an' 'e was bleedin' – 'e 'ad a big gash across 'is leg. The old lady told me there was a vet she knew who lived up the road and could I take Mr Hargreaves to 'im, quickly. She's infirm, you see – bad legs. She was so worried 'e'd die, 'er only friend. So, I said I would, an' I did. I ran across the road, jumped through the 'ole in the side fence and ran across the park for a short cut. On the way, Mr Hargreaves, the poor little blighter, was cryin' an' strugglin' and that must 'ave bin when I lost me glove – such a nice pair, too. Me Auntie Alice gave 'em to me for Christmas an' I really didn't want to lose 'em.'

Boase stood up and walked to the window. What a mad story this was turning out to be.

'And what happened to Mr Hargreaves?'

'Well, 'e's still at the vet's, but 'e's 'ad an operation and 'e's goin' to be just fine.'

'And will this old lady ... um...'

'I still don't know 'er name, – might be Bea or something – I don't know, I'm sure; it all 'appened in such a rush. But, do you know, she was so grateful, when I told 'er about me gloves, she even insisted on giving me the money for a new pair.'

'That was very kind of her. But she, and presumably the veterinary surgeon, will be able to verify your story?'

'Well ... yes, I'm sure they will – why, am I in some sort of trouble? You 'aven't even told me why I'm 'ere.'

Bartlett drained his cup.

'A man was found murdered in Kimberley Park yesterday...'

'Oh my Gawd – an' you think *I* 'ad something to do with it?'

'I didn't say that, Miss Parsons, but we have to explore every avenue, you understand.'

'Yes, of course. Can I go now?'

'Yes, you may. My superior would expect me to detain you but I'll be keeping an eye on you. Be kind enough to give your address, the old lady's address and the veterinary surgeon's details to the desk sergeant, would you? And if you know or hear anything more about this you must let me know immediately. Understand?'

'Yes, I will – an' I 'ope you catch the murderer. Blimey, 'e could 'ave 'ad me an' Mr Hargreaves, an' no mistake.'

Sheila Parsons left the office and went to the desk in the lobby. Boase closed the door behind her.

'Well, sir, she's a bit of a character. Why did you just let her go?'

'Harmless enough, I should think, but we need to check her story – just go to the desk with her, make sure she doesn't pull a fast one, she might know something. We can't afford to slip up now,

Boase. If she's right, of course, the blood came from the cat. Seems a bit of a tall one, but they sometimes are. Get someone on to it, will you? I can't believe all this, Boase; what a terrible, terrible crime to find on our own doorstep.'

At nine o'clock the next day, Boase, not wishing to leave such an important job to one of the juniors, jotted down the details of the veterinary surgeon which Sheila Parsons had left at the main desk. His note read:

Aloysius Bone, Veterinary Surgeon
81, Dracaena Avenue, Falmouth

Boase stuffed the note into his pocket and took the fifteen minute walk to the surgery. The sign on the door indicated that Aloysius Bone was open for business and Boase walked into the small waiting room. On one seat was a rather large lady wearing an impossibly small hat. Boase smiled to himself, thinking how funny she looked. On her enormous lap was a basket from which emanated the most irritating feline wail. On the seat next but one, for there was not enough room for anyone to sit right next to the large lady, was a very small man in a dark grey suit. He had enormous white hair and a tiny, trim moustache. On the floor at his feet lay an Irish Wolfhound which was so large and had such long legs that he covered most of the small waiting room floor. Boase stepped carefully over the dog's paws and rang the brass bell underneath the *'Reception'* sign. A frosted glass window opened in the wall and a young girl of about sixteen appeared.

'Can I help you, sir?'

Boase coughed, cleared his throat and replied, 'I'd like to see Dr Bone, please.'

'I'm sorry, he's busy in his surgery at the moment – and it's *Mr* Bone.'

'Oh, I'm very sorry. I'm from the local police and I wanted to ask Mr Bone about a young woman who brought a cat here early on Saturday morning...'

'Oh, Mr Hargreaves, have you come to collect him?'

'I'd really like to speak to Mr Bone.'

'Well, as I said, my father's busy at the moment and these clients are in front of you.'

Boase turned and looked at the large lady and the small man and looked at the Irish Wolfhound and listened to the wailing cat.

'Would you mind if I waited?'

'No that's quite all right – take a seat.'

'Thank you.'

Boase hesitated and, wondering where he could find room to sit, decided to stand outside the small waiting room. As he stood, he wondered about the murder in the park. How did the body get there? If Desmond Cook was brought to the park, having being murdered somewhere else, why wasn't there a trail of blood? Moreover, where was the man's head? As Boase turned things over and over in his mind, the young girl tapped him on the shoulder.

'My father can see you now.'

'Thank you very much, miss.'

Boase followed the girl back inside and into a small room which appeared to double as a consulting room and operating theatre. The length of one wall was occupied by two large metal cabinets with countless gleaming instruments contained therein. In a corner was a large lamp about six feet tall and, next to it, a smaller one. In the centre of the room was an adjustable table and on another wall, several anatomical charts and diagrams. Under the window, at a small wooden desk, sat Mr Bone. He stood up as Boase and the girl entered the room.

'Good morning, sir, I'm Constable Boase from the police station; I was wondering if I could have a brief word with you?'

Mr Bone shook Boase's hand.

'Of course, what about?'

'I need to query your treatment of a cat on Saturday morning – it would give support to someone's story. You understand I can't elaborate...'

'I understand. Are we talking about Mr Hargreaves?'

Boase smiled.

'Yes, we are – strange name for a cat.'

'You hear all sorts of names in my profession; makes you wonder what these people call their children.'

Boase agreed. He had quickly taken to the large Scot with his deep voice and broad accent.

'You see, sir, a young woman said she brought Mr Hargreaves to you on behalf of an elderly neighbour and I just need proof that what she said is true.'

'Well, yes it is. The lady gave her name as Sheila Parsons. In fact I know Mr Hargreaves of old. His mistress is a lady called Mrs Bumble Toy. She's quite old now and I've been treating her cats for several years. I think Mr Hargreaves is about the fourth or fifth she's had. It seems that she asked Sheila Parsons to bring him because he'd had an accident. She can't get out much, you see. When the girl arrived, the poor little chap was in a terrible state. Looks like he'd gone through a wire fence or something like that – maybe even a broken window – and that caused a very large gash across his leg. Lucky he didn't cause himself more damage.'

'So there would be quite a lot of blood then?'

'Plenty, no doubt about it.'

'Thank you, sir, you've been a great help. Oh, just one more thing – is it possible to distinguish positively between animal blood and human blood?'

'This is all very intriguing, Constable. Yes, it is possible.'

'Even dried blood?'

'Even dried blood.'

'Thank you very much, Mr Bone. Goodbye. Goodbye, Miss Bone.'

Boase made his way back to the police station. Bartlett was in his office and the younger man relayed the conversation he had had with the veterinary surgeon. Bartlett listened and smoked his pipe.

'So, if we establish that the blood on Sheila Parsons's glove is that of Mr Hargreaves, we can believe her story?'

'Looks that way, sir.'

'Good, well you can sort that out, can't you, Boase?'

'Right oh, sir. Leave it to me. Anything else?'

'Yes. We ought to contact these two ne'er do wells from young Cook's student days ... um...'

Bartlett rummaged through a large pile of papers on his desk.

'...um, Charlie Wentworth and Leon Romanov – thinks he's a relative of the royals, does he? All very strange that, Boase. We need to arrange to speak to them. Also, when the other Cook boy returns from Egypt, we should speak to him too. Don't know how close the boys were but he might know something. I'll check on the whereabouts of the chums – is that what the upper classes call them – chums?'

'I'm sure I don't know, sir,' replied Boase, trying not to laugh. He'd never met anyone so entirely working class and who had no time whatsoever for those who had everything. Bartlett was a grafter all right and believed that if you wanted something, you had to work for it.

The twelfth of August came and went marking one week since the discovery of Desmond Cook's body. Few further clues had been turned up. Sheila Parsons appeared to have been telling the truth when the blood on her glove proved to be that of Mr Hargreaves. By the next day Bartlett had tracked down Wentworth and Romanov and he and Boase would travel to Oxford to question them.

'We were lucky, Boase. When I got a reply from the Wentworth boy he said that Romanov was coming to see him anyway this week so that kills two birds with one stone. Must admit, I don't fancy going to

London in this sweltering heat – I had enough of that when I was young. You wouldn't believe the stink coming from some of those factories in the old days. I've seen people keel over in the street during the summer, completely knocked out by the heat. Did I ever tell you I used to walk past the vinegar factory every day ... that smell will stay with me forever, terrible it was. Now, Falmouth, well, that's a different kettle of fish altogether; all that lovely fresh, sea air, you don't know when you're well off, Boase.'

Boase was secretly disappointed that the London trip was off – he'd been once before with Bartlett, only for a short time when they were working on a previous case, but he really wanted to spend some more time there; it looked so exciting, all those buildings and the number of people was unbelievable, all rushing everywhere, so busy. Of course, he wouldn't want to live there, no, a day or two was more than enough he thought. But, yes, he'd like to go there again – maybe next time, Irene would go with him. For now, though, he would have to be content with Oxford.

Chapter Three

The next day, as the day before, dawned hot and sunny. Bartlett and Boase were installed on the train bound for Oxford, wondering what information Wentworth and Romanov might be able to give them. Both men dressed in civilian clothes as demanded by Greet. Bartlett was aware that Greet didn't like spending money on things like travel – he thought it was wasteful but he agreed that it was preferable to calling in detectives from London and if Bartlett and Boase could solve a crime then it made life easier. There wasn't much time though. Bartlett hoped something would come of the visit; there was not much to go on so far, besides, he wouldn't return home until the next day and he so hated leaving Caroline overnight. He sat back in the seat and watched the countryside rush by the window and thought of his son, John; how he still missed him. What fun they'd had when he was a boy, fishing, flying kites, digging potatoes – all the ordinary things most fathers did with their sons. And now, well now it was all gone, just memories of another lifetime, another world. Bartlett's thoughts were ended suddenly as he felt a jab in his ribs.

'Pork pie, sir?'

'No, thank you, Boase. How you can eat the things you do amazes me. Pork pie, at this time of the morning? I'm gasping for a cuppa though. When you've finished that, perhaps you could go in search of some tea.'

'I've just got one more boiled egg to go, then I'll be with you, sir. When I come back with the tea, perhaps you'd like a piece of fruit cake – Mrs Curgenven packed loads, even more than *I* can eat.'

'I find that rather hard to believe, somehow,' murmured Bartlett, half under his breath.

The two settled down for the journey ahead.

Bartlett dozed as the sun concentrated its rays on the window of their compartment. Boase eagerly watched everything passing by and marvelled at how the countryside and the towns changed in different parts of the country – how unlike Cornwall it was, even different things grew in the hedgerows. By the time the train pulled into Oxford, Bartlett was exhausted and hungry. He and Boase alighted and made for the station exit. The older man lit his pipe.

'Right, Boase, the address is 5 Becket Street – here's a map, have a look.'

As Boase checked whether Becket Street was within walking distance, Bartlett sat on a wall and looked amazed at the number of men walking around in their shirt sleeves – and thought how they'd never have done such a thing in his day.

'It's here, sir, look, just by this station. It shouldn't take us more than about two minutes to walk.'

'Right, that's lucky, let's go then.'

The two men began walking, enjoying the sunshine and the new surroundings. Boase decided he liked the look of Oxford very much. Within minutes they turned into the road known as Becket Street and quickly came to number five. It was a large, Victorian, four-storey house of red brick with front steps and precariously balanced terracotta pots containing summer flowers of every colour imaginable. Bartlett rang the brass bell and the two waited. A figure appeared in the hall and could be clearly seen through the glass paned front door. The door opened and a woman stood there, looking enquiringly. She looked to be in her fifties, was very tall and thin and wore her dark brown hair in a long plait which reached her waist. Her dress was pale green silk and looked to Bartlett that it would cost him a year's wages to buy anything like that for Caroline.

'Yes, can I help you?'

'Good morning, Madam. I'm Inspector Bartlett and this is Constable Boase – we have an appointment to see Mr Wentworth.'

'Which one?'

'Oh, forgive me, Mr Charlie Wentworth.'

'That's my son – I'm Annabel Wentworth, do come in.'

The thin woman held out a bony hand, first to Bartlett and then to Boase.

'He has a guest staying from London at the moment. Wait here please and I'll fetch him.'

They had been led into a large drawing room at the front of the house. Velvet chairs were lined regimentally around the sides of the room and an overbearing fireplace with an extremely ornate mantelpiece formed the focal point of the room. Bartlett and Boase sat down with a spare seat between them. Boase felt like he was at the doctor's surgery. At the far end of the room stood a large, ugly, mahogany sideboard and on it a tantalus next to which something green was growing in a pot which even Bartlett did not recognise. There was a strange aroma pervading the house; Bartlett thought it was some kind of drug that had been recently smoked. Presently they heard several sets of footsteps and the door opened. Mrs Wentworth stood there.

'Charlie is here, gentlemen, and his guest also –

would you like some tea?'

Boase stood up.

'Tea would be very nice, thank you Mrs Wentworth.'

'Please, you must call me Annabel, I insist.'

Boase nodded acceptance but felt very uneasy with the arrangement made by the thin, strange woman. As she left, the two young men entered the room. The first walked over to Bartlett.

'I'm Charlie Wentworth – I got your message. I'm devastated, I can tell you. Poor old Desmond.'

Charlie Wentworth had a very young-looking face – he looked about sixteen. Bartlett wondered how anyone would take him seriously as a solicitor; he didn't even look old enough to shave. Tall, like his mother, he was very blond with sharp, blue eyes and a mischievous air. He was dressed for golf.

'Forgive my clothes, won't you, Inspector Bartlett – we were just waiting for you to turn up and then we're off; I'm teaching Leon the game. Oh – I'm frightfully sorry. Let me introduce my friend.'

The other man stepped forward from the doorway where he had been listening to the conversation. He was, in contrast, short, round, and dark-haired, with strange tortoiseshell glasses that made his eyes look very peculiar. Boase found himself staring. The foreign gentleman offered his hand to Bartlett and spoke in a strange drawl.

'Good afternoon, I am Leon Josef Nikolai Alexei Romanov, at your service.' At this he bowed very low.

Boase stared harder. Now Bartlett was staring too. Was this man real or were they in some mad dream – or in a terrible play? Leon Romanov wore a suit that looked to date from about 1870 and carried a small cane on top of which perched a gold parrot. As he smiled, two large teeth protruded over his top lip.

'I'm pleased to meet you. We've come a very long way today to speak to you about your friend, Desmond Cook – we really hope you'll be able to help us.'

Bartlett led Charlie Wentworth out into the large hall while Boase tackled Leon Romanov. They spent about twenty minutes speaking to the two men about Desmond Cook and, after bidding farewell to Mrs Wentworth and thanking her for the tea, they headed towards the centre of Oxford for something to eat. The Cadenza Restaurant looked like a reasonable place overlooking a small park.

'You must be starving, Boase, why, you haven't eaten for at least ninety minutes,' quipped Bartlett.

'You're right, sir, I *am* feeling a bit peckish.'

The two men found themselves a window seat in the Cadenza, which was very clean and modern.

'I hope the food's better than the décor,' mumbled Bartlett removing his coat, 'I suppose this is the latest thing – what do they say, *with it?* Or "all the rage," as my Irene would say.'

'I think it is, sir, I like it very much.'

'Hmmmmm, bit sparsely furnished, if you ask me.'

A young waitress arrived to take their order. Bartlett was pleased to see that the menu wasn't 'with it' and ordered roast beef with Yorkshire pudding and vegetables, followed by treacle pudding with custard. Boase, after changing his mind several times and keeping the waitress shuffling from foot to foot, chose haddock with boiled potatoes and green beans with plum tart to follow. The two tucked in and ordered a small glass of beer each.

'Can you believe it, Boase, no Leonard's, and we're not a million miles from London, are we?'

'No, sir. Anyway, gives you a chance to try something else – a change is as good as a rest.'

Bartlett, unconvinced, sipped the drink, made a strange face, and continued to eat.

'Anyway, my boy, let's talk about those two oddballs – you first.'

'Well, sir. That Russian is a bit of a strange one all right. I've never met a Russian before. All he could tell me was that Desmond had loads of friends, particularly ladies – apparently everyone was jealous because of the number of women he was always with. He was very generous and kind, the sort that'd do anything for anyone. Very gifted academically too. He had plenty of time for everyone and was the life and soul of the party. All in all, it seems that he was a very nice sort of chap and got on with most people – particularly women.'

'Mmmmm, wonder what the attraction was?'

'Don't know, sir. Anyway, all he said was that he didn't think Desmond had any enemies. He was always fun, very outgoing – not a hard worker, mind. Didn't do particularly well in his examinations – not because he wasn't intelligent, rather he was lazy. Just scraped through at the end by all accounts. He also asked about Donald – asked if he'd been told the news; he said the cousins were quite close – although they weren't studying at the same time or in the same college, they sometimes came here to parties. I think Romanov knew Donald quite well.'

'Strange,' Bartlett finished his meal and lit his pipe, 'that's not the general idea of things I got from Charlie Wentworth.'

'Oh?'

'Well, *I* was told, same as you, that he had loads of women friends but also that he was always in debt. According to Wentworth, he was always borrowing money, even though his father had set him up very nicely. It seems that young Cook was a bit of a gambler and, if Wentworth is to be believed, he borrowed to gamble and gambled to pay for some drug habit – talking of which, did you smell something odd inside that house earlier?

'Well, yes, it was a bit queer,' Boase replied, 'what was it?'

'Mark me – some kind of drug, I'd say – yes. I've smelt stuff like that before. Don't know what exactly, but definitely drugs. Anyway, Wentworth said he practically sat Desmond's examinations for him come the end. He had to go into his room every morning to wake him up and get him dressed. Cook was invariably drunk or drugged up – and pretty bad-tempered too, hardly any time for anyone mostly. There was barely a stick of furniture in his rooms and few clothes. Wentworth himself even lent him money – twenty pounds, would you believe – never had it back. When I asked if he thought anyone would want to kill Desmond Cook, he replied, "almost everyone, I should think,” so, it seems, that if all this is true, Charlie Wentworth was more of a friend to Desmond Cook than Leon Romanov, or whatever his blasted name is. Anyway he gave me some more names of people that Cook owed money to but couldn't tell me where they are now – they've all gone their separate ways. So, what do you make of that, Boase?'

'I really don't know, sir. It's all a bit puzzling. How can we get two such different accounts of the same man?'

Bartlett and Boase settled their account at the Cadenza and left for a small guest house they had managed to arrange. By the time morning came, the two, still exhausted from their travels the day before, just boarded the train in time for the return journey. Later that day, Bartlett turned his key in his own lock. Topper had refused to sleep in his basket all night and lay on the mat by the front door; he was still there, dozing, one ear listening. As soon as he heard his master's key turn, he was up, overjoyed at his return. Topper had missed his late night walk and no doubt wondered why his beloved master had not returned. Bartlett patted the dog's head.

''Ello, Topper, old boy – you bin a good lad for your mother? No, no, I'm shattered old man. We'll go out later, now you go and lie down again, go on, get into bed. Good lad.'

Topper obeyed and settled down into his basket. The house was quiet. Bartlett looked in the kitchen – there was a note from Irene which was propped up against the milk jug.

Dear Dad
Just gone to the shops, Mum's having a nap.
Some sandwiches and cake on the dining table.
Love Irene xx

Bartlett crept upstairs to his bedroom; Caroline had left the door open – something she didn't usually do. Perhaps she had felt nervous. Bartlett sat on the edge of the bed. Caroline turned.

'George, is that you?'

'Of course it's me, princess – I hope you weren't expecting anyone else?'

'Don't be silly, I'm just a bit sleepy.'

'Don't get up, princess. I wouldn't mind a quick cuddle though, I'm all in. That's quite a train journey you know.'

Caroline sat up anyway and gave Bartlett a hug.

'Did you get on all right?'

'Well, not as much as I'd hoped, but it wasn't a complete waste of time, I'm sure.'

Bartlett gave his wife a kiss.

'Topper wouldn't go to bed last night. He slept on the mat – he really missed you.'

'I know, he was lying there when I came in. He's in his basket now.'

'I missed you too, George.'

'Ditto.'

Bartlett and Boase, barely refreshed, made some attempts at work but achieved little for the rest of the day. Deciding that useful production would come after a good night's sleep they packed up and resolved to come in extra early the next day.

Greet was still watching Bartlett closely and time was now their enemy as far as he and the London police were concerned.

When Bartlett set off the next morning he still felt as though he'd had no sleep at all. He'd been up by half past five and taken Topper for a short walk. The dog had looked disappointed when Bartlett had turned halfway to return home.

'I'm getting too old for all this, Topper, boy. Come on, we'll go out again tonight – promise.'

When Bartlett reached the police station, he looked at his pocket watch; fifteen minutes to seven. Good. There'd be time for a cup of tea while he discussed the case with Boase. As he walked up to the door he could hear a loud angry voice coming from the lobby. He walked in to find a man shouting at Constable Penhaligon and Boase. The man was about forty years old, wearing a pair of navy canvas trousers, a navy jersey, and a black woollen short coat. He wore light deck shoes.

'I'm telling you, you've got to listen to me. For God's sake. It was terrible. I can't believe it. I'm even handing myself in to make you see it's true. Please – you've got to do something.'

Bartlett walked across to the man.

'Would you like to come into my office, sir? You're getting overwrought. Penhaligon, make three cups of tea please.'

'Right away, sir,' replied Ernest Penhaligon, thankful to be relieved of his current task.

Bartlett showed the man into his office and offered him a seat.

'Now, calm yourself and tell me what all this is

about, upsetting the whole station like this.'

Boase sat down and waited – he had only just arrived minutes before Bartlett and could make no sense of the tale either.

The man took a deep breath.

'Well, you see, sir, it's like this – an' I 'ope there won't be no repercussions, 'cos I 'onestly 'ad nothing to do with all this – I just found it – right?'

Bartlett sat back in his chair and sighed.

'Would you *please* start at the beginning, man – here you are look, a nice pot of tea. Now, please begin.'

'Well, you know you bin lookin' for the Trawlerman?'

'Yes, we have – what of it?'

'Well. You see, sir, it's like this ... well ... it's ... it's me. *I'm* the Trawlerman.'

'YOU?'

Bartlett and Boase looked at each other.

'Yes, it's me, and I've got a very good reason for telling this to you.'

'Go on, tell.'

'Well, this morning, I 'ave to confess to you that I was burgling someone's 'ouse – early this morning, when I found a terrible, terrible thing. I 'ad just pinched some silver plate from a room upstairs – an' a very nice set it was too, me mother always wanted something as nice as that, God rest 'er soul...'

'Go *on,* man,' Bartlett was becoming impatient.

'Well. I picked up all this lovely set an' me bag wasn't big enough – jewellery is what I normally go for most, but, well, I couldn't really leave something as nice as that, could I, so, over in the corner of the room was a sort of ... big, grey bag, I thought it'd do nicely to put me spoils in. Anyway...' the man broke off and began to shake.

Boase handed him some sugary tea.

'Drink this, sir, it'll help.'

The man took a couple of large mouthfuls.

'Well, when I opened the bag to put the stuff in, there it was ... *in the bag!*'

'What was?'

'A man's 'ead.'

'Oh, my God,' Bartlett sprang to his feet. 'Quick man, the address – quickly.'

'It was at number fourteen, Bar Terrace – but what about me? Aren't you going to arrest me?'

No reply came. The two men had already left the room and the door had slammed shut. Boase stopped at the desk in the lobby where Penhaligon was speaking on the telephone.

'Penhaligon – don't let that man leave ... he's the Trawlerman! Get someone to fetch Greet to deal with him. We've got to dash!' Bartlett stuck his head back through the front door.

'Boase, hurry up, get a car.'

Within five minutes, Bartlett and Boase had arrived at the large house in Bar Terrace. Bartlett repeatedly rang the bell until the door was opened. A young boy of about nine stood there.

'Young man, are your parents at home?'

'No, sir, there's just me an' me little sister.'

'Well, when will your father be back?'

''E's be'ind you.'

Bartlett and Boase turned to see a tall man walking up the path towards them.

'What's goin' on 'ere then?'

Bartlett hurriedly introduced himself to the man, eager to get inside the house.

'I need to search your house, I have reason to believe that there is evidence here of a very serious crime and I'll thank you not to stand in my way.'

Before the man could argue, Bartlett and Boase had entered the building and were on their way upstairs. Bartlett took the first bedroom, Boase the next. Within a minute, Bartlett called out.

'Boase, he was right, it's here.'

Bartlett came out of the room, carrying the bag described to him by the Trawlerman.

'It's here all right, Boase. Get this fellow's details, will you?'

Bartlett took the bag and its contents outside and waited in the car while the stunned owner of the house sat on the front step. Boase sat next to him.

'I'm sorry about this, sir, but, you may know a very serious crime was committed recently and we're working on the case.'

'The murder in the park?'

'Exactly. What's your name, sir?'

'Penfold. Jim Penfold.'

'And this is your house?'

'Yes.'

'Who lives here with you?'

'Well, there's just me an' the kids. My wife died about fifteen months ago – she 'ad tuberculosis...'

'I'm sorry, sir.'

'Well, we'd only just moved in 'ere the year before, after me mother-in-law died. She left us the 'ouse. It was always too big so we started letting out some of the rooms. Six bedrooms is far too much. Me wife was from a big family an' she grew up 'ere. I s'ppose it was all right for thirteen children, but not for us. Ann always wanted to sell it, but it was 'er fam'ly 'ome an' I didn't think we should. Silly really – the money would 'ave bin 'andy. Now she's gone I can't bring meself to part with it. It reminds me of 'er. I still see 'er ev'rywhere, you know. So, I carried on taking in lodgers; that means I can work part-time in the docks and still look after Stephen and Angela.'

'Have you any lodgers at the moment?'

'No – I had two dockers until yesterday, but they've gone now, Swedish they were. Oh, and one other; a young woman, she left last night.'

'Do you have the Swedish gentlemen's addresses?'

'I'm sorry, no. They only stayed a couple of nights. People always pay me in advance, so I don't like to pry.'

Boase had thought this would be too much to hope for.

'What about the woman?'

'Oh, yeah, I know 'er name. Bit 'ard not to really, she never stopped talking the 'ole time she was 'ere. Nice girl. She was called Sheila Parsons – from up country ... London.'

'Sheila Parsons! Are you sure about this?'

'Of course I'm sure. Lovely girl, very talkative – she played with Stephen and Angela a lot. They really liked 'er. She wasn't 'ere long. I think she 'ad lodgings somewhere else before but she 'ad to leave – like I said, I don't like to pry.'

'Do you know where she is now?'

'No idea, sorry, like I said...'

'Yes, you don't like to pry. Right, sir. I need to ask you about that bedroom. Who usually sleeps in there?'

'No one – it's just a spare. It's the smallest so I don't usually let it out to anyone.'

'And when were you last in there?'

'Probably about a week ago. There's a box on top of the wardrobe where Stephen and Angela keep some old toys and they asked me to get it down for them; yes, about a week ago.'

'Is it normally locked?'

'Why would it be?'

'Just wondering. So any of your lodgers could go in and out of that room at any time?'

'Well, I suppose so – but why would they? There's nothing in there.'

Boase thanked Jim Penfold and walked back to the car where Bartlett was waiting.'

'I've put it in the boot – at least we've found it. We'll have to send it off and have it examined. Any luck with him?'

'Not really, sir, but something interesting came up.'

As they drove back to the police station, Boase told Bartlett about Sheila Parsons.

The same evening, Boase was at the Bartlett's house again. Irene had asked her father to invite him for tea. At six o'clock the four sat down at the table to a light summer meal. Sandwiches, cold meat, puddings, and cakes.

'Look, Archie, I've made you some pork pies – Dad says you really like them.'

Boase felt embarrassed.

'Well ... er ... yes, I do, Irene. Your father's quite right – and they look lovely.'

The four sat and ate and Bartlett and Boase had a couple of Leonard's.

'Do you know, princess, in Oxford, you can't even get Leonard's? Who ever heard of such a thing? Well, one thing's for sure – we *won't* be moving up there.'

'Not everyone likes Leonard's, I'm sure, dear.' Caroline smiled at her husband.

'Then they must be mad, that's all I can say – isn't that right, Boase?'

Boase was secreting a large piece of the delicious pork pie under the table to a waiting Topper who received it gently and gratefully.

He whispered to the dog, 'Good boy, Topper. Was that nice? It's the nicest pork pie I think I've ever tasted.'

'My Irene's a good cook and no mistake about that, Boase.'

'Dad,' now it was Irene's turn to look embarrassed, 'it's only pork pie.'

'Nothing wrong with being able to cook good, wholesome, English food, nothing at all. You should see the stuff they eat abroad. I was reading only the other day ... listen to this all ... in some countries they eat *dogs* and *cats* – who ever heard of such a thing. Unbelievable, I say.'

'We eat animals too, George.'

'That's different, princess. Dogs are for companions, not tables.'

Topper, now full of pork pie, let out a huge sigh under the table.

'That's right, Topper,' Boase patted the dog's

head, 'don't you listen to things like that, cover your ears. Why's he called Topper, sir?'

'Well, my boy, when I was a young man, new to the force, I was sent on an errand to Hyde Park police station and they had a little fox terrier there, lovely he was. He was called Topper. He used to go out with the constables – more company than use I think, but he was such a dear little chap, so intelligent. I've never forgotten him and I always said that when I had a dog I'd call him Topper.'

At this, the dog crept from under the table and licked his master's hand.

'You're a good 'un, Topper, old boy, you really are.'

Caroline stood up.

'Well, you two, it's still early. What are you going to do now?'

'Don't know, Mum. What would you like to do, Archie?'

'I don't mind – you choose.'

'Well, we could go to see a film. Harold Lloyd is showing – if you'd like to.'

'Why not? Get your coat.'

The two left the house and walked to the town. Reaching the St George's Hall in Church Street, they joined a long queue.

'Do you mind waiting, Archie?' Irene asked as she slipped her arm through his.

'Not a bit, Irene.'

As Bartlett and Boase drank their first cup of tea at the police station early the next morning, Penhaligon rushed in with a large, brown envelope.

'These are the postmortem reports on Desmond Cook, sir. The courier said to tell you it's very urgent.'

'Thank you, Penhaligon.'

Bartlett tore open the envelope and scanned the contents.

'No, no, *no.* This can't be.'

'What, sir, what's happened?'

'NO!'

'What, sir?'

Bartlett jumped up from his chair, throwing the report across the desk to Boase.

'This says that it's impossible for the severed head we found to belong to the body of Desmond Cook. There's no way they could match up. *The head belongs to another body!'*

Chapter Four

Bartlett and Boase sat, lost for words. Boase sipped his tea, Bartlett stared out of the window. At last, Bartlett stood up.

'Well, we all know what this means, my boy – there's been another murder. And, if I'm honest, I don't know where to start with this one, indeed I don't.'

'Sir, is there any way that this could be a mistake?'

'No, it's definitely right, lad. Definitely right. We need to go back to the drawing board with this one now, right back to the beginning. So, what do we know already?'

'Well, sir, Desmond Cook's body was found decapitated in the park–'
'Are we now sure it's his body, eh?'
'I suppose we aren't, sir.'
'Right, well, that's the first thing we need to find out – the body had no documents or money – absolutely nothing. Dr Cook recognised the clothing but maybe we shouldn't have placed so much on that. The clothes were right, his usual location was right but that's not enough now, is it? Try to sort that out, will you, Boase? We need to talk to Sheila Parsons again, also that man Penfold at Bar Terrace – oh, and maybe Dr Cook. We have no time to waste. Perhaps you could do Parsons and Penfold – I'll take the doctor. Do we know where that young woman is?'
'She said she wasn't leaving yet the last time I spoke to her so she'll be around, sir. I'll find her.'

Boase arrived at the large house on Bar Terrace. He rang the bell. No reply. He knocked. No reply. Thinking that someone might be in at the back of the house and couldn't hear him, he walked around the side garden to the rear door. As he reached a kitchen window he heard a sound coming from inside; he stopped and listened. He could hear two people laughing – a man and a woman. He quietly approached the window and looked inside. At the far end of the room a woman was cooking and a man had his arms wrapped tightly around her waist. Boase looked closer. Both people had their backs to him but he could easily see that it was Jim Penfold and Sheila Parsons. Boase was aghast. He rushed across to the back door and knocked loudly. The noise inside the house stopped and footsteps approached the door. After a hesitation, it was opened and Jim Penfold stood there.

'Constable Boase?'

Penfold was clearly surprised and invited his guest inside.

'We're in the kitchen,' Penfold added, somewhat reluctantly.

Boase followed him into the room where Sheila Parsons still stood at the cooker. She looked up as the two men entered.

'Oooh ... you're that policeman, aren't you? I recognise you from the other day.'

'I didn't expect to find you here, miss?'

'Well, no – that is, I was leavin' for London tomorrow, but then I changed me mind.'

'And why was that?'

Penfold stepped forward and put his arm around Sheila's shoulder.

'I asked her to, Constable Boase. When Sheila was staying 'ere, well, we got quite attached to one another. She left, as I told you, but came back because she thought she forgot something yesterday – that's when I asked her to stay. She didn't really 'ave anywhere else to go and I think I'd like the company, so, 'ere she is.'

Boase was puzzled by this unexpected turn of events.

Jim Penfold sat down on a chair by the back door.

'What is all this about, Constable Boase? We 'aven't done nothing wrong. You and your boss come bursting in 'ere the other day, like a pair of lunatics, asking all sorts of questions and searchin my 'ouse – what for? I 'aven't killed anyone. Now you're quizzin' us cos we've decided we might like to spend some more time together – I really don't see what that's got to do with anyone 'cept us.'

Sheila Parsons never spoke.

'No, well,' Boase leaned against the pantry door, 'it wouldn't normally be anyone's business, but, following our previous visit to you, we have now discovered that we are not dealing with a murder any longer...'

'You've caught 'im then?' Sheila fiddled with the buttons on her cardigan.

'I didn't say that, miss – nor did I say the murderer was a man. I was about to tell you that following our last visit here, we are now dealing with *two* murders.'

'Well, what's that to do with us? I told you everything I know when you came here – and 'ow did that visit lead you to 'aving two murders now?' Jim Penfold was beginning to get angry at the events happening in his kitchen.

'Let's just say that I've come back because we previously found an item in your house that tells us that two men have been murdered; that's all I can say for now. But I would like you to tell me anything else that you've overlooked. It's very important.'

At that, Stephen and Angela came running through the passage and entered the kitchen. They ran to Jim and hugged him.

'Well, I've told you all I know – and I'm sure Sheila 'as too...'

Sheila nodded and said nothing.

'So please leave us alone now, Constable Boase.'

'Well if you feel you've forgotten anything, please call into the police station and ask for me or Inspector Bartlett? Oh, and – both of you, please stay nearby ... this enquiry is so large that you'll definitely be spotted if you try to leave the town.'

Boase left by the same back door and entered the garden. As he walked around to the street he puzzled over what had just happened. None of it made any sense.

Bartlett was already at the station when Boase returned. He relayed what had just happened at Bar Terrace.

'Well, that's strange all right, Boase. I thought Sheila Parsons had left Penfold's place?'

'That's what he told us, sir, but apparently she came back.'

'Right, well, I don't mind saying, I'm well and truly stumped – where do we go from here? Oh, there is one thing, just a minute.'

Bartlett was fumbling in his pocket.

'Greet's just been in here – he nearly had a seizure ... I'm surprised you didn't hear him shouting when you were at Bar Terrace. Look, Dr Cook left this message with his maid. It says that Desmond had a house which he sometimes used, although he mainly lived at Florence Terrace. He says here that he doesn't have a key though. We should go round there and see if we can find anything.'

'What's the address?'

'Er, 2, Windsor Terrace – that's up the back of Killigrew. We'll get over there – failing anything there, any other ideas, my boy?'

'We could try Donald Cook tomorrow – isn't he docking tonight? Maybe he could tell us something about Desmond.'

'Well, yes, but what? He's been out of the country – what could he know about all this business? No one's been reported missing, we've got two separate body parts belonging to two people and I don't know what to do.'

Bartlett mopped his brow with his handkerchief and stared out of the window onto the street below.

At the doctor's surgery on Florence Terrace, Ingrid Cook sat in the dining room with her husband. In front of her was a bowl of thin soup. She turned it over and over with the spoon, pausing only to dab her eyes with a handkerchief.

'Ingrid, darling – please try to have a little soup. You need to stay strong now, Donald will be here tomorrow and he'll need you too. *I* need you. Please have just a little.'

'I really can't face it, dear. I think I'll go up now.'

Dr Cook glanced at the mantel clock. It was only a quarter to eight.

'My dear, could you please make me a dose of that sleeping medicine, only I do rather think it beneficial – and as you say, Donald will be here tomorrow and I need to rest.'

'Of course I will – but, Ingrid, you mustn't take things like this in place of your food – you need nourishment...'

'Yes, but I need sleep too. Oh, I forgot, will you be near Arwenack Street tomorrow at all?'

'Well, not tomorrow, no, but definitely the day after – you know I visit old Dr Skinner there each week. Is there something I can fetch for you? Will it wait until then?'

'Yes, please – and yes, it will wait. Would you pop into Bendix and Hall to collect my bracelet? I had it altered – it was a little on the large side. Donald brought it back for me last time and he'd like to see me wear it, I'm sure. It's so pretty – and apparently very valuable. I'll get you the alteration receipt before you leave. Did you know he's bringing me something else? I always ask him not to but he does anyway. The bracelet is beautiful and it's more than enough. He wrote to me and said he has a dear little gold ring – look at this letter, he's even made a small sketch of it.' Ingrid withdrew an envelope from a concealed drawer in the underside of the dining table and held it out to her husband. He took it and noted the contents and the sketch.

'He thinks the world of you, darling – and he appreciates everything you've done for him over the years; let him spoil you if he wants to.'

Ingrid kissed her husband on the cheek and went up to bed.

Boase had made a visit, on his way home, to Windsor Terrace. There was no way to easily gain access. All the downstairs curtains were drawn and no neighbours could offer any information. At nine o'clock the next morning, he brought Bartlett a cup of tea.

'We'll have to break in, sir. I had a good look round – that's the only way.'

'Right. Finish your tea – we'll go over there now.'

The two men made their way across to Killigrew and, reaching St Mary's Church, crossed to Lister Hill and into Windsor Terrace. A few people were walking by and so Bartlett and Boase made their way around to the back of the house. There was a locked gate which led into the garden. Boase pushed it and it gave a little. He went at it again with his shoulder and the gate was open. He went into the little garden, followed by Bartlett.

'There's a small pane here, sir. Look, just above the latch to the scullery door.'

'Might be locked with a key, though.'

Boase had already broken the glass and was reaching down for the bolt. He drew it back, turned the knob and the door opened.

'You got lucky there, Boase.'

The pair entered. There was a small scullery, a kitchen, and a parlour.

'I'll have a look upstairs, sir.'

Bartlett was left in the parlour. He opened a couple of drawers in a desk. They were empty. The room was sparsely furnished. No photographs or pictures on the walls. It looked like it was just a part-time accommodation. Boase came back downstairs.

'You should see up there, sir. I've never seen anything like it.'

'What do you mean?'

'Well, let's say, it looks like whoever was here last knows how to throw a good party. There's definitely been a woman up there – or two.'

'I'm sure I don't know what you're talking about, Boase.'

'Neither do I really – just looks like someone has been up there and, unless Desmond liked wearing women's clothes, I'd say he'd had a few lady friends.'

'That's enough of that kind of talk Anyway, we already knew he liked the women – that's obviously what this place is about. I can't see his parents approving of his behaviour. Find anything useful?'

'Not a thing.'

'Me neither. Waste of time. Still, we had to check.'

Disappointed, the two left by the scullery door, Boase making good the window before he closed the door.

At three o'clock in the afternoon Dr Mortimer Cook, having finished his morning surgery and his house calls, was waiting on the platform at the railway station; he was happy to be seeing Donald but so very sad at the news he was going to break. He lit a pipe and wandered up and down the platform in the warm afternoon sun. He turned over in his mind how he was going to tell Donald what had happened. The truth was, he didn't really know himself what had taken place, other than his son had been horribly murdered and no one had yet been caught. The police knew nothing. He looked at this watch. Five more minutes. He could hear the train coming down the line now. He straightened his waistcoat, tugged his cuffs slightly and watched as the train came towards the station.

There was a sudden surge of people leaving the

train, doors banging, suitcases being trundled back and forth, people shouting. Dr Cook watched everyone. Hands being shaken, hugs and kisses exchanged. A large dog, barking loudly, broke loose from the guard's van and bounded along the platform, and almost knocking down a small child who instantly screamed and ran to her mother.

Then the station fell silent.

Dr Cook stood on the platform.

'Maybe he decided on a later train, dear,' Ingrid Cook offered helpfully, 'or maybe tomorrow. Yes, he'll come tomorrow.'

'Well, he never said,' replied her husband, not looking up from his newspaper.

'He might have just missed the train from London and has to wait until tomorrow. I'm sure we'll hear exactly that.' Ingrid busied herself winding some wool, in a way thankful that they had some more time to work out how to tell Donald their awful news.

Dr Cook did not feel the same; he wanted it over with.

George Bartlett walked over to the window and opened it wide. It was only eight o'clock in the morning but it warm already. Boase sat at his desk watching him.

'Cheese sandwich, sir?' He offered a small paper bag.

'No thank you, Boase. What's going on with Sheila Parsons? We've got nothing to suggest she's involved in the Park murder but yet, here she is, shacked up with a man who already told us she'd left – in the very house where we find a man's head in a bag. What's all that about, eh?'

'Well, I don't know, sir, but as Jim Penfold already pointed out, they're not doing anything wrong. I suppose he's got pots of money and she probably knows it but that hardly makes her a murderer.'

'Quite.'

Bartlett finished his tea. As he drained the cup, the telephone rang.

'Yes, yes, I understand – well could there be any other explanation? Is there any way of contacting him? Are you sure there's not some mistake? All right, I'll see what I can find out. Try not to worry, I'm sure there's no need. Thank you, goodbye.'

Boase looked at Bartlett enquiringly.

'That was Dr Cook – he and his wife are panicking a bit because their nephew was supposed to arrive back from Egypt yesterday – he went to the station at three but no sign of him. He'll probably turn up today. They're naturally worried because they wanted to tell him about Desmond and now they think he's had an accident or something. Anything we can do, Boase?'

'Well, I'm not really sure, sir. Have they got the dates right?'

'He says so.'

'Well, I've got five minutes later on so I'll see what I can find out.'

'Thanks, Boase – be sure to let them know if you hear anything?'

'Of course, sir.'

'Yes, thank you very much, Mr Bosustow – yes, you've done a marvellous job, as always. My husband will be so pleased. Now, how much do I owe you?'

Quentin Bosustow, the manager of Bendix and Hall jewellers in Arwenack Street, was a short and stout man of about sixty who always wore a black suit with a black waistcoat and a blue silk necktie. He bowed to his customer and reached under the counter for a small pad of paper. He quickly scribbled some calculations and looked up over his horn-rimmed spectacles.

'Well, Mrs Ingleheart, shall we say eleven and sixpence – would that be acceptable?'

Dr Cook, waiting at the counter, suddenly felt overwhelmed by the heat and sat down on a chair near the open door of the shop. He pondered over whether to come back later on for his wife's bracelet – there was still another customer in front of him and if she was as complicated as Mrs Ingleheart he might be here for some time. As he contemplated what to do, Mrs Ingleheart took her repaired jewellery and left the shop. He stood and lifted his hat as she passed by him. A young woman was now at the counter. She looked in a hurry, which suited Dr Cook. She handed something to Quentin Bosustow and muttered urgently. The jeweller removed his spectacles and, slowly lifting a small glass to his eye, peered at the item he had just been given.

'Well, miss, well, it's not something we would normally deal in – this isn't really my area of expertise. Of course, I can see it's gold and I could offer you something for that...'

The woman became more agitated.

'Well, how much ... how much can you give me?'

'Well, now let me see ... shall we say three pounds?'

'*Three pounds?* Only three?'

'Miss, Egyptology is the latest thing at the moment, I understand that, but to me the only real value would be in the actual gold...'

The woman leaned over the counter, snatched the piece of jewellery and ran out of the shop.

Dr Cook, who had been listening to the exchange, approached the counter.

'Yes, sir, can I help you – oh, it's Dr Cook, isn't it? Oh, my dear sir, can I say to you how very sorry I am to hear of your recent and most terrible bereavement.'

'Thank you, Mr Bosustow – but can you tell me, what was that young woman trying to sell you just then?'

'She was offering me an Egyptian ring – very nice but only worth the gold value to me ... seems to be that she was looking for quite a bit more than I was prepared to pay...'

'Have you a pencil, Mr Bosustow?'

The jeweller offered the pencil and Dr Cook drew on the small paper pad which was still on the counter. He replicated the sketch in Donald's letter to Ingrid and handed it back to Mr Bosustow.

'Did it look like this at all?'

The man behind the counter looked hard at the drawing.

'But, but – how could you know this? That's incredible.'

Dr Cook didn't wait to reply. He fled from the shop, looking up and down Arwenack Street. The woman was nowhere to be seen.

Constable Penhaligon knocked at the door of Bartlett's office and entered, carrying a brown envelope.

'This is for Constable Boase, sir.' He handed it to Bartlett.

'Thanks, Penhaligon – I'm a bit parched, you wouldn't put the kettle on I suppose?'

'No problem sir – be right back. Shall I make one for Constable Boase, sir?'

'Yes, thank you, I'll think he'll be back directly.'

At that moment, Boase arrived.

'Yes, I wouldn't mind, Penhaligon – thanks.'

'This just arrived for you.' Bartlett handed over the envelope.

Boase tore it open and scanned the contents.

'Blimey, sir ... listen to this. This is from the shipping office at Southampton. Donald Cook left Alexandria almost a month ago ... looks like he docked back in England on the first of August, according to their timetables. But Dr Cook was only expecting him this week.'

'So where can he be – and where has he been?' Bartlett was turning his unlit pipe over in his hands.

'Good morning, I wish to speak with Inspector Bartlett please.' The Russian accent came as a surprise to the desk sergeant taking this telephone call at Falmouth police station.

'Who shall I say, please?'

'Please to tell him my name is Leon Josef Nikolai Alexei Romanov and I am at his service.'

'Please wait a moment.'

The desk sergeant tapped on Bartlett's door.

'Sir, could you take a telephone call?'

'Yes – who is it?'

'Well, sir, I tried to write it down – look, here you are sir.'

The desk sergeant handed Bartlett a small slip of paper on which he had attempted to write the caller's name. Bartlett looked at it then, removing his reading glasses, looked at the messenger.

'Well, yes, all right then – I'll take the call.'

'Inspector George Bartlett here. How can I help?'

'Oh, Inspector Bartlett, good morning – it is I, Romanov.'

'How are you, sir, what can I do for you?'

'I am worried, Inspector – about my friend Donald Cook. I have telephoned to the house of his uncle and he has told me that he does not know where Donald is.'

'Do you have any need to be worried, sir?'

'Well, yes, I think so.'

'What do you know?'

'Well, I am not sure – you see I have just received a letter from Donald...'

'Donald? Go on.'

'It was posted in London on the third of August. In it my friend says he is worried that someone is trying to kill him.'

'Does he say who this might be?'

'No, nothing other than since he arrived back in England he is sure that someone is following him.'

'And what is your opinion of this?'

'Well, all I know is that Donald often carried valuables around with him – Egyptian artefacts ... sometimes jewellery. Maybe someone was trying to rob him, yes, but why would he think that someone was trying to kill him? I wish I had known – I might have been able to help him – I do not understand why this letter has come to me only now. He says he is staying with friends in the East End of London before he returns to Cornwall – he mentions a woman he met on the return journey from Egypt.'

'Any names?'

'No, none.'

'Right, well, thank you, sir, I must ask you to keep in touch if you hear any more that might be of interest to me.'

'Of course. Goodbye.'

'Goodbye, sir.'

Bartlett replaced the telephone receiver and turned to Boase who had been listening to the one side of the conversation.

'Guess that was the Romanov?'

'Yes ... said he had a letter from Donald. Apparently he thought someone wanted to kill him – felt like he was being followed.'

Boase sat down and drew a piece of paper from his desk drawer. He licked the end of a very tiny pencil and wrote down:

What do we know?
Desmond Cook murdered 05.08.23
Donald Cook returned from Egypt 01.08.23
One body found. One head found. Two people
Donald Cook should be here – he isn't

Rising from his chair, Boase screwed the paper into a ball and threw it into the waste paper basket.

'Don't do that, Boase.' Bartlett retrieved the paper and straightened it out. He looked at it spread before him on his desk.

'What were you thinking about when you wrote this?'

'Well, I was thinking, wouldn't it be good if there was a way of telling if people were related just by their – I dunno, their blood or something?'

'Related? What are you thinking – the same thought that crossed my mind not twenty minutes ago?'

'Well ... I'm thinking ... wondering, if the two partial bodies we found are both Cooks...'

'I didn't dare venture to suggest it, Boase, but ... it could make sense.'

Chapter Five

Arthur Pouch folded up the *Falmouth Packet* and lay it neatly on the breakfast table. The headline uppermost read: *Still no clues for Falmouth police in body in park murder.*

Arthur Pouch had lived in Falmouth all his life, since 1860. Since 1860 he had never uttered a word, well, not that anyone could remember and so, it was assumed that he had never spoken since birth. He lived alone in a small house at the top of Jacob's Ladder, a flight of one hundred and eleven steps rising up from the Moor. He was a small man and walked rather like a little bird, often stooping to pick things from the ground – particularly discarded rubbish, which he hated to see on the street and so he would collect it all, take it home and burn it on his fire. Children mimicked him when they saw him, strutting and bending down like a chicken. He ignored them.

His one treat was to have a drink in the Star and Garter Inn at the top of High Street and he was regularly seen there gazing out of the window across to Flushing. No one had any idea of how many years he had been doing this but everyone recognised him and offered him a smile or a wave when they saw him.

Arthur finished washing up the breakfast things and looked again at the paper on the table. He opened it and reread the story about the murder. He removed his little wire spectacles and thought for a minute or two; replacing them, he read again. There was a picture of the two Cook boys – one murdered, the other, apparently missing. He recognised them. But from where? They looked familiar to him but he couldn't imagine how or why. The paper replaced once more on the breakfast table, Arthur Pouch pulled on his old coat and left the house for his usual walk around the town and to buy himself some tobacco and two ounces of humbugs. He walked for over an hour when he found himself at the tobacconist's shop by the docks. Having completed his purchases and stooped to pat a friendly little terrier tied to a rail outside the shop, Arthur began his walk back home. As he turned the key in the lock, something came to him. Why, of course! Those two young men were in the saloon bar the very night before one of them was found murdered in the park. He had seen them with his very own eyes. But, oh, how terrible. Such a ghastly murder. And what of the other boy? They say he's disappeared. Yes, indeed, such a terrible business.

Archibald Boase looked at the clock in the office he shared with George Bartlett. Next he looked at his watch. Rising from his chair, he crossed to the door, opened it and addressed Constable Penhaligon.

'Penhaligon, what time do you make it?'

The constable looked at the clock above the door.

'It's almost half past one – it's past your lunch time, isn't it?'

'That's exactly what I was thinking,' replied Boase and returned to the office. Opening a canvas haversack which he had pulled from under his desk, he removed a large paper bag. He laid it in front of him.

'Mind if I have my lunch now, sir?' He looked across at Bartlett.

'No, you go ahead – I wouldn't like to see you starve, would I?'

Boase had already opened the bag to reveal a very large pasty. Bartlett watched him.

'Your landlady make that?'

'Yes, sir, yes she did.'

Boase took out a small knife and made a jagged cut across the pasty. He offered the smaller part to Bartlett.

'Corner, sir?'

'No thanks, Boase, you enjoy it – you're wasting away as it is. Can't imagine why – you got worms or something?' The older man was grinning. Boase ignored him. No one was going to interrupt his pasty.

Penhaligon knocked at the door and entered.

'Sir,' he addressed Bartlett, seeing Boase was otherwise engaged, 'Dr Cook just telephoned and wondered if you would be good enough to call at his surgery sometime later today. He really wants to speak to you but his wife is unwell and he doesn't want to leave her just at the moment.'

'Did he say what it was about?'

'No, sir, he wouldn't say, but that he would explain everything when he saw you.'

'Right you are, I'll call round later ... fancy a walk, Boase? You might need to walk off all that pastry.'

Bartlett and Boase arrived at Dr Cook's house and, having knocked, waited on the step. The doctor opened the door and invited them in.

'Thank you for coming to see me – I'm sorry I couldn't come to you but my wife is feeling very unwell and distressed. Donald's apparent disappearance is upsetting her greatly.'

'No need to explain, sir – how can we help you?' Bartlett sat down on a chair by the window.

'Well, I'm puzzled about Donald not arriving – he's usually fairly reliable and, to be perfectly honest, Inspector, well, I'm beginning to worry.'

'Well, that's understandable, sir, in the light of everything that's happened–'

'Yes, but there's something else.' Dr Cook interrupted.

'Go on, Doctor.'

'Well, it's all rather strange really. You see, Donald is always in the habit of bringing something back from his travels for us – well, mostly for my wife. You can see how much stuff we have from Egypt in the house. Personally, I wouldn't give you a thank you for it but, well, Ingrid likes it and so I tolerate the gestures. Well, the other day, Ingrid showed me a letter she had received from Donald in which he said he was bringing her a ring. She put the letter away and thought no more of it. She asked me to go to Bendix and Hall, the little jewellers, you know. She wanted me to collect a bracelet which Quentin Bosustow was repairing for her – she so wanted to wear it when Donald arrived home; it was a gift from him after his last trip. I'm sorry, where are my manners – can I give you some tea?'

'No thank you, sir. Please carry on.' Bartlett was becoming curious now – he hoped this story would end up in a clue to his investigations.

'Well, look, here's the letter – I asked Ingrid if she minded my showing it to you and she gladly gave it to me. Here's a little pencil sketch of the ring he's bringing.'

Bartlett searched for his reading glasses and Boase stood behind looking over the older man's shoulder.

'Yes, I see, sir. But I don't understand...'

'I went to Bendix and Hall yesterday for the bracelet. It was rather busy – and warm so I sat by the door waiting my turn at the counter. Well, the first customer paid her bill and then something very strange happened...'

'Go on, Dr Cook.' Bartlett and Boase exchanged a glance hoping for something useful here.

'A young woman approached the counter and tried to sell something to Quentin Bosustow. She was obviously dissatisfied with the price he was offering and she quickly left the shop. When I approached him, he said it was an Egyptian ring but he would only pay her the price of the gold – no more. Something came into my head – I don't know how or why but I replicated the little illustration you hold there and showed it to him. He couldn't believe it. Of course, it's obviously unique – that, he said, was the exact ring he had been shown minutes before. Naturally, I ran after the young woman – but she was gone.'

Boase was startled by this.

'So, what you're saying, sir, is that the young woman in Bendix and Hall had the ring belonging to Donald and which he was about to present to your wife on his return?'

'Yes, that's exactly what I'm saying.'

Bartlett leaned forward on his chair.

'Well, this is a bit of a surprise, Dr Cook. Tell me – can you describe this woman to us?'

'Yes, I can – she had bright red hair and wore men's trousers and an overcoat ... even in this searing heat.'

Bartlett rose from his seat.

'This may be very important and useful, sir, thank you. Will you please let us know if you hear from Donald?'

'Yes, of course I will. I'll show you out. Thank

you for coming. So, you think this information is relevant?'

'Well, it's something to go on, definitely. Thank you, sir. Good day.'

Bartlett and Boase walked back through Dr Cook's garden. Neither said a word until they were at the end of Florence Terrace.

Boase spoke first.

'Well, that's a turn-up, sir? What's it all about?'

'I'm not sure, Boase. That ring, Dr Cook says, is unique and the jeweller recognised it from his sketch. If that's so, someone got that ring from young Donald Cook. And we think we know who the young woman with the red hair and men's trousers is, don't we?'

'Sheila Parsons,' both men uttered at the same time.

The next two days dragged by slowly and Greet had, after a heated confrontation with Bartlett, agreed to grant an extra few days.

'You understand, of course,' Greet had said, 'that this is only on account of a shortage of men up in London for the foreseeable – yes, if it wasn't for that, you'd be off this case long before now, George.'

Bartlett didn't care – he just wanted more time. He *did* care, however, about being called George by Greet – as if they were friends. They worked together, that was all; friends they would *never* be.

The August heatwave continued and Bartlett and Boase were making slow progress. Sheila Parsons had also vanished and the pair had had no luck in tracing her.

Bartlett sat by the window at his desk and lit his pipe.

'Irene said she wouldn't mind a picnic tomorrow, Boase – don't know what she's got in mind ... fancy tagging along?'

'If you're sure that would be all right, sir. Thank you – I'd like that very much.'

'Well, I don't like missing my Sunday lunch, I admit – but Caroline said we could have something on Monday instead, so that's all right. Why don't you come to the house at midday tomorrow?'

'Thank you very much, sir. I will.'

So it was that on Sunday afternoon, the small party of George Bartlett, Caroline, Irene, and Archie Boase, accompanied by Topper, were sitting on the beach at Swanpool tucking into a cold lunch. The sun was beating down and swimmers, walkers, and boaters were everywhere, it seemed to Bartlett.

'Now, don't get me wrong all – I love this little town and the coast and the lovely air, but, well, all these people, I can't bear it. Look at them, half dressed...'

'George, do stop,' Caroline threw a napkin at him which landed on his head and Boase and Irene had a fit of giggles.

'Oh, Dad – these people are only having fun, I'm sure lots of them are on holiday. You must know how good it feels to escape the city air.'

'Well, yes, I'll grant you that, Irene. I wouldn't mind another one of those ham sandwiches, if there's one going?'

The four, and Topper, ate sandwiches, cake, and fruit, and drank several cups of tea. Topper began to dig nearby in the sand and barked triumphantly when he turned up a broken doll. He brought it across and dropped it at Bartlett's feet.

'Well, thanks, boy – that's an interesting thing to find.'

Topper barked and moved back some distance indicating he wanted to play 'fetch.'

Bartlett obliged and the game continued until boredom set in on both sides.

'Would you like to go for a little walk, Archie? We could get an ice cream if you like.' Irene stood up and held out her hand to Boase. He stood, brushed the sand from his trousers and, patting Topper on the head, took Irene's hand. They walked in the direction of the cliff path to Gyllyngvase.

Caroline sat closer to Bartlett and put her head on his shoulder.

'I think they make quite a nice pair, don't you, George?'

'Well, yes I do – don't know why they don't get on with it though. There's no need for Irene to stay at home for our benefit, is there?'

'I agree – but you know what she's like. They'll do what they do.'

Bartlett kissed his wife on the top of her head and took a piece of fruit cake. He was enjoying the day but, if he was honest, he didn't feel good relaxing like this when he had so much work to do.

The day grew cooler. Irene and Boase returned arm in arm, seemingly very happy in each other's company and the four packed away their picnic ready for the walk home. Topper ran back for his doll and dropped it into the open basket.

Arthur Pouch locked his front door and stuffed the front page of the *Falmouth Packet* into his pocket. Walking slowly and holding onto the handrail, he made his way down Jacob's Ladder. Crossing the Moor, stopping only to pick up a sweet wrapper and deposit it in the litter bin, he continued his way to the police station. He was greeted by Constable Penhaligon. The two had known each other since Penhaligon was a boy.

'Hello, Arthur. You all right today?'

Arthur Pouch nodded and, taking the newspaper from his pocket, pointed to the picture of the two Cook boys. He tapped the paper with his finger then tapped the side of his nose.

'What, you know something about this, Arthur?'

The old man nodded and pointed to the sign indicating Bartlett's office.

'Wait a minute – have a seat.'

Arthur sat and Penhaligon knocked on Bartlett's door. Boase, who had just been on his way out for some tea, opened the door and bid Penhaligon to enter.

'Come on in, Penhaligon, what is it? I was just after some tea.'

Bartlett was standing looking out of the window. He turned.

'Sorry to bother you both, but Arthur Pouch is

outside. He's got a newspaper article with him – the one with the photographs of the two Cooks – he wants to see you.'

'Well, bring him in then.'

Arthur Pouch removed his hat and entered the office.

'Good morning, Mr Pouch – I hope you're well,' said Bartlett offering the man a seat. A nod was the reply. The man indicated by a writing gesture that he needed a pencil and paper. Boase brought it for him. Ten minutes passed and Bartlett and Boase watched, intrigued, as the old man wrote out three pages in very large handwriting. He bent over the work and despite Boase's best efforts he could see nothing until the essay was complete. Having finished, Arthur Pouch handed the pages to Bartlett. Silence ensued all round while it was being read.

'This is very interesting, Mr Pouch – very interesting. Are you sure about this?' The old man nodded and then nodded more, his hand on his heart.

'Well this is really very kind of you and helpful too. I can't thank you enough. Would you like a cup of tea before you leave?'

Arthur Pouch shook his head but stood up and, taking Bartlett's hand in his, offered up a very firm handshake, and then the same to Boase. He replaced his hat and left.

Boase had almost turned himself inside out trying to discover the contents of the pages.

'Come on, sir. Share.'

'Well, you'll find this very interesting, Boase. I

certainly do.'

Bartlett showed the newly gained information to his assistant. Boase sat at his desk, incredulous.

'So, let me see if I understand this, sir. Arthur Pouch was in his usual seat in the Star and Garter when he witnessed all this? That's unbelievable. So this girl he says he saw ... let me see, he describes her as having bright red hair and a very loud voice – but not with a local accent. So that has to be Sheila Parsons. She's turning out to be a bad penny. Now these three men she was talking to ... who are they?'

'Well, Boase, we know they must be the two Cook boys – Pouch says he recognised them when he saw them in the paper – but who's the other one she was so chummy with? That's what we need to find out.'

Bartlett and Boase took a walk up to the Star and Garter. It was closed. They went around the back where a door was open. Bartlett went up the two steps.

'Hello, hellooo – anyone in?'

A middle-aged man with grey hair and a rather large stomach, around which was tied a black apron, came to the open door.

'Well, if it isn't Mr Bartlett. Hello, sir, how are you?'

'I'm all right, Enrico. How's business?'

'Very good, thank you for asking. And who is this handsome young man?'

'This is my assistant, Archibald Boase. Archie – meet Enrico Trewavas.'

The two men shook hands.

'Can I get you a drink, gentlemen?'

'No thanks, Enrico – we're working.'

'Oh, please – just a small beer on the house?'

'Well, it is rather warm – go on then ... you've talked us into it.'

The three men went into the empty saloon bar where Arthur Pouch was accustomed to sit. Enrico Trewavas poured two glasses of beer and set them down on the table. The landlord was well known to Bartlett – he had helped him greatly with information relating to a previous case in his early days in Falmouth. His Cornish father had met his Italian mother many years before, married her, and brought to this part of the world.

'So, do you need my spying skills again, Mr Bartlett?' Enrico chuckled.

'Well, in a way, yes, I do. You must have heard all the murder talk around the town?'

'Oh, yes, I have. Terrible, terrible, that poor boy.' At this point, Enrico made the sign of the cross across his body. 'It's hard not to hear gossip in my job, Mr. Bartlett.'

'I hoped you'd say that.' Bartlett sipped his beer.

'Well, you know I was there the day they found him.'

'Really?'

'Well, yes, I had just come out of mass when I heard all the trouble. I had walked down the side of the park to come back here. I stopped – Valentina felt sick and we paused by the top gate until she felt a little better. I heard that young woman screaming. I felt so sorry for her when I discovered what she had found.'

'Someone has told me that not only was Desmond Cook drinking in here the night he was murdered but that Donald was too. Did you notice anything unusual about them when they were in here?'

'You're probably wondering why I didn't tell you that Desmond was in here ... well, simply because there was nothing to tell.'

'But can you think of anything now, Enrico?'

'No, not really – I had no idea until you just told me that the other man he was with was Donald Cook. I suppose, thinking back, they looked similar – but youngsters do these days, don't you agree, Mr Bartlett?'

Bartlett stood up and walked across to the bar.

'Well, I suppose they do, but maybe that's just because we're getting older, Enrico. Where were the Cook boys standing?'

Enrico showed the place at the bar.

'Now, Enrico, think carefully. Who else was with those two lads?'

Enrico Trewavas stared into the distance, his brow furrowed.

'Well, now, there was someone ... a young, red-haired woman; yes, that's right, and a man.'

'What was the man like?'

Enrico thought again.

'Well, he seemed quite short, greasy, black hair – and he had a gold tooth, I remember. Yes, he was with the girl.'

'Right, now, this is really important. Did the man and woman leave here together, what time and did they leave before or after the Cook boys?'

'Wait.'

Enrico opened the door behind the bar and called out.

'Doreen. Doreen. Could you come down, please?'

Footsteps were heard on the stairs and a woman appeared behind the bar. She was about fifty, rather overweight, with greying hair tied up in a bun.

'Mr Bartlett, do you remember my wife, Doreen?'

Doreen stepped forward.

'I remember you, Mr Bartlett – how are you?'

'And I you, Doreen. I'm very well, thank you. This is Archie Boase, my assistant.'

'Pleased to meet you, Archie Boase.'

'Doreen,' Enrico patted his wife's hand, 'do you remember the night that Desmond Cook was here? The night he died?'

'Why, yes, I do. He'd had one or two too many as I recall.'

'He was drunk?' Boase stared hard at the woman. 'How bad?'

'Well, he was upright but I told him he should go home and sleep it off. Oh! Mr Bartlett, Mr Boase, is it my fault he was murdered?'

Bartlett put his hand on the woman's shoulder.

'No, of course it isn't, Doreen. How could it be? You mustn't think that at all. Now, please, tell me about anything unusual that happened that evening in this bar.'

Doreen stepped behind the bar and poured herself a glass of lemonade. She sat on a stool at a table by the window.

'Well, Desmond came in with another man...'

'That was Donald Cook,' her husband said.

'Oh, no, not the poor boy that's gone missing? Oh, his poor family. Well they were together, chatting and drinking.'

'Can you remember what they were talking about, Doreen?'

'Well, the man, Donald, was telling Desmond about Egypt, I think. Yes, he was saying he'd come back early to England and had spent a few days in London.'

'Go on.'

'Well, that's all really. He seemed to be trying to persuade Desmond to go back again with him – to Egypt. Desmond said he couldn't afford the ticket.'

'Now, your husband says there was a man and a woman with them?'

'Well, yes, well, not with them – they came over to the two young men halfway through the evening.'

'Can you remember when the four of them left?'

Doreen frowned.

'Please, Doreen, it's so important.'

'Well, I told Desmond he had drunk too much and I gave him a glass of water. Then Donald said he was leaving and he would see Desmond the next day.'

'What time did Donald leave?'

'Quite late, for us. We had trouble getting everyone out – so he left at about eleven o'clock.'

'And the others?'

'The man and woman left a couple of minutes after that and then I sent Desmond on his way at about twenty past eleven.'

'Anything else?'

'No, I'm sorry, no.'

'Well, thank you both so much for your help – and the beer. Please let me know if you hear anything else that you think might be important, Enrico?'

'Yes, of course, Mr Bartlett, of course we will.'

Bartlett and Boase left by the back entrance and down the small flight of steps. As they reached the bottom, Doreen Trewavas called after them.

'Mr Bartlett, Mr Boase, there *is* something else ... I don't know if it's important.'

The two men returned back up the steps to the door.

'What have you remembered, Mrs Trewavas?' Boase really hoped something here would be helpful to them.

'Donald had a ring...'

'Go on, what about the ring?'

'He was showing it to Desmond when he was telling him about Egypt. Desmond looked at it and handed it back. That's all really.'

'So, did Donald have the ring the last time you saw it?'

'Yes.'

'Thanks, Doreen.'

Chapter Six

Sheila Parsons rubbed her eyes and yawned. Leaning across the pillow, she picked up her watch and squinted to see the time. Half past seven. She listened. She could hear birds singing in the garden and, downstairs, the sound of Jim Penfold cooking breakfast. Stephen and Angela were fighting in the garden. In different circumstances this would be heaven for Sheila Parsons – but no, this was more like hell. OK. She'd do it. She'd tell the police everything she knew. She couldn't live like this, backwards and forwards, hiding away and, besides, she'd be doing them a favour and perhaps they'd feel sorry for her and she'd be safe. Safe. That wasn't something she felt at the moment. What she would give to feel safe right now.

The bedroom door opened and Jim Penfold came in carrying a tray of kippers, toast and a pot of tea.

''Ere you are my lovely, I brought you some breakfast and a nice drop of tea.'

'Thanks, Jim. What have I done to deserve this special treatment?'

'I'm just very 'appy to 'ave you 'ere, that's all. Oh, and I'm 'oping you'll go into the garden when you've finished and sort out Stephen and Angela – they're getting on me nerves. I told them they 'ad to share the bicycle but Angela's been on it for nearly an hour...'

'An hour? But it's only 'alf past seven now.'

'They both got up early to try to get the bike first.'

Jim smiled and lifted Sheila's pillows so she could sit up and eat.

'Right, I'm off to work now. I'll see you later.'

Jim patted Sheila's hand and went out on to the landing, leaving the door ajar.

'Jim ... Jim.' Sheila called out. Jim stuck his head back around the door.'

'Yes, my lovely? What is it?'

Sheila dismissed him with her hand.

'Oh, it's – it's nothing. Don't work too hard. Bye.'

The man disappeared down the stairs and Sheila could soon hear three voices in the garden below the open window.

'Yes, but Angela, you've been on it all the morning. You must let Stephen have a turn. Why don't you go in and have some toast? Here you are, now, Stephen – you can have 'alf an hour and don't go on the road. Sheila will be down in a minute. You could ask if she'd like a walk on the beach, couldn't you?'

Sheila listened and soon heard the bicycle crash to the ground, its bell tinkling as it landed, accompanied by Angela's sobs and hurried footsteps into the scullery. She lay back on her pillows and sipped some more tea.

Alice Vyvyan stood on a small wooden table and peered through the open window of the Seven Stars. Inside, her father, Binny, was trying to have a quiet drink.

'Please Dad, can I go – everyone else will be there. Please?'

'No. I don't know any of the people there and I don't know the man you're goin' with. I've 'eard stories about these so-called private parties and you're not goin'. That's my final word, Alice.'

'Dad.' The earlier voice of reason became a whine.

'Daaaad. It's a really big birthday party. Everyone else is goin'.

'Alice, if I get up out of this chair and come outside, you'd better not still be standin' there. I've said no and yer mother's said no. So, *no*.'

Alice Vyvyan jumped down, kicked the table, and, trying not to look like she'd hurt herself, stamped across the Moor to where she'd left Sam Jackett waiting.

'It's no good, Sam, Da says no.'

'Well, maybe ask 'im tomorrow – the party's not till Friday.'

George Bartlett lit his pipe. He looked at the clock and then at his watch – could it really be only three o'clock he thought. He looked across at Boase.

'What do you make of this business about the Egyptian ring, Boase?'

'Well, it's a puzzle right enough, sir. How did Sheila Parsons get it?'

'I can't fathom it either.'

'I can't help thinking, sir, that the head we found is Donald Cook. Does that sound completely mad?'

'Well, no, not mad. But it was in such a bad state that there's not really any way of telling for sure ... looks like it'd been burnt or something. – presumably to disguise the identity? I don't know – if you believe that someone could wilfully do something like that then you have to believe anything. I suppose we'll hear back soon enough – last I heard they were having real trouble making any sort of identification.'

'Well, I can't sit here all day – if you don't mind, sir, I'm going back to Bar Terrace to see if Sheila Parsons has turned up. I've been up and down that road two or three times a day at various times but I haven't spotted her yet. I think she must still be there but avoiding us. Is it worth calling in at Bendix and Hall to ask about her there ... she may have brought the ring back?'

'Why not – yes, you go, Boase – come straight back afterwards, Greet wants to see us both.'

'Oh no.'

Grabbing an apple from his desk drawer, Boase left the office and went out into the street.

Approaching the parish church, Boase was delighted to see Irene on the other side of the road.

'Irene ... Irene.'

He ran across the road just as Irene turned around.

'Hello, Archie – how nice to see you. Aren't you working?'

'Yes, well, I'm just on an errand actually. How are you?'

'I'm very well – in a bit of a hurry though ... I'm on an errand too, I've got to take these groceries to Mrs Angove – do you remember her? She lives at the end of our terrace.'

'Yes, I do – the old lady who always sits in the window?'

'That's her. She's got very bad arthritis so I usually call in to see if she needs anything if I'm going past. Her son is visiting her today and she hasn't seen him for almost a year – I think she said he lives in Dorset. She wanted me to get some fancy biscuits and some cake.'

'That's really very kind of you.' Boase thought how considerate Irene always was to everyone; she was such a lovely person.

'Well, if you'll excuse me, Archie – I really must go.'

'Of course, Irene, I'm so sorry to hold you up – but I'll see you again soon I hope?'

'Of course.'

Boase awkwardly leaned forward to kiss Irene's cheek just as she bent down to pick up her shopping basket. Their heads collided.

'Oh, Irene, I'm so sorry – are you all right?'

Boase retrieved the basket and put it into her hand. She giggled.

'Of course I'm all right. Why don't you just kiss me goodbye?'

She looked at him and he quickly pressed his lips on hers.

'Bye, Irene.' And he was gone, blushing.

Arriving at the Penfold place, Boase found no one to be at home. No Jim Penfold, no Sheila Parsons, no Stephen and no Angela. He walked around the back of the house – the back door was locked and all the windows were closed. Boase peered into the kitchen and the scullery. There was no one around. He resolved to keep returning or maybe send a junior policeman until he'd found her. He returned to the front of the house and left through the garden. Bendix and Hall might be worth a try – maybe Sheila Parsons *had* tried to sell the ring again.

Just over an hour later, Boase returned to the office. Bartlett was refereeing an altercation between two men who had been brought in for brawling at Greenbank. Eventually, deciding that he was getting far too old to deal with this, he called Penhaligon and Coad, the latter only in the job for four weeks, and retreated to his own office.

Boase was looking out of Bartlett's window.

'You could have lent a hand there, Boase.'

'Well, I could see you had the matter in hand, sir – you were dealing with it admirably.'

'Don't get chippy with me – I had to leave before the volume increased any further.'

'Sir, do you know that man down there?'

'What man?' Bartlett walked over to where Boase was standing at the window.

'Look, that man across the road.'

'Well, what's wrong with him – he's just waiting for someone probably.'

'Loitering more like – looks a bit shifty to me.'

'Haven't you got anything to do, Boase – tell me about your walk to Bar Terrace and then we have to see Greet. Oh, there you are – look, he's gone. Anyway, I haven't had a chance to say to you that Irene looked in about twenty minutes ago – said something about a private birthday party that everyone is going to ... I think she's hoping you'll take her.'

Boase perked up.

'*Everyone*, sir? That's an awful lot of people.'

'Her words, not mine. Anyway when you see her perhaps you could arrange it – if you want to go, that is. I don't even know whose party it is but I know she'll be in good hands with you.'

Boase took this as a compliment and the two men went to the upstairs office to see Greet.

The following day as Boase took the walk to the police station from Melvill Road, he resolved to call on Irene later that day to ask about the birthday party. He didn't really care who would be there or what the occasion was – he just wanted every opportunity to be with Irene. As he turned onto Killigrew Street he stared ahead of him. There was a woman about a hundred yards in front of him – the bright red hair was unmistakable. That was Sheila Parsons all right. Boase ran at top speed, crossed the road and found himself at the corner of Clifton Place. He looked up and down the road. She had vanished. A grubby, short man stood at the entrance to Albany Road, watching the proceedings. Boase called to him.

'Hey, you! Did you see a woman with red hair just come past here?'

The man didn't speak but shook his head and walked off up Albany Road.

Boase continued on to the police station. He stopped at the entrance. That man – yes, he thought he recognised him. He was the one loitering across the street yesterday. Boase had never seen him before and now twice in quick succession. He carried on into the office where Bartlett was making some notes for Greet.

'Sir, you'll never believe this – I just saw Sheila Parsons in Killigrew Street. I ran after her but she'd gone and then I saw that odd man who we saw from your window.'

'Right, Boase, don't take off your coat – let's try Bar Terrace again, she must go back there some time – she told us she had nowhere else to go.'

As the two men left by the front door Boase tugged Bartlett's sleeve.

'Look, sir, it's her – over there.'

Sheila Parsons was walking quickly on the other side of the road.

Bartlett called to her.

'Miss Parsons, Miss Parsons.'

The girl looked across and waved – not a casual or friendly wave, rather an indication for the men to wait for her. She ran across to them.

'Blimey, I'm so pleased to see you – I was just on me way 'ere. I 'oped you be in ... looks like I almost missed you.'

'Well, you've led us a merry dance, Miss Parsons, and no error. Boase has been looking for you everywhere.'

'Well, now you've found me and I really need yer 'elp.'

The three went inside the police station and sat down in Bartlett's office.

'You'd better begin, Miss Parsons – what did you want to see us about?'

Bartlett lit his pipe and sat back in his chair. Boase perched on the corner of the desk – he wanted to make sure he heard everything that this young woman had to say.

Sheila Parsons looked nervous as she spoke.

'I 'aven't really bin 'onest with you.'

Boase looked at her.

'Well, yes, we guessed that. Go on. We need to know everything. What do you know about the two Cook boys? Start with them.'

'Right, well, I knew Donald cos I was working on the ship to Egypt. 'E was travelling back to England and 'is was one of the cabins I 'ad to caretake. At first I thought 'e was a bit of a toff but 'e used to talk to me about all sorts of interesting things – like Egypt and Oxford ... 'e knew so much about everything. Well, anyway, when we got back to England 'e wanted to meet some friends in London before 'e came 'ere to Falmouth. So, since 'e'd bin so nice and friendly to me, I offered for 'im to stay at a place near me – in Bethnal Green.'

'But you could have told us all this before – you really should have said something. This is a very serious investigation, Sheila.' Bartlett looked at the young woman.

'I know. Well, I was scared you'd think I 'ad something to do with that 'orrible murder and I didn't know what to do – so I just kept 'iding away. Jim's bin so good to me – you won't let anything 'appen to 'im, will you?'

Both men ignored the question – how could they know what Jim Penfold's involvement had been?

Boase put his hand on Sheila's shoulder.

'Go on – what else?'

'Well, I didn't see Donald after we got to London 'e just went off, I assumed to see his friends. 'E'd told me so much about Falmouth when we were on board the ship and I'd 'eard that there was a job going 'ere – which was what I told you before. So, I came down on the train for the interview – I didn't really 'ave anything to keep me in London and I arrived 'ere on the Friday. The rest is as I told you. I didn't get the job, I decided to stay for a few days and then I met Jim.'

Bartlett tapped his pipe on an ashtray.

'Tell us about the evening in the Star and Garter, Sheila.'

Sheila fidgeted. She didn't know that anyone had told of that evening.

'Well, there's not much to tell, really. I was 'aving a drink in there and chatting to Donald – 'e was surprised to see me and 'e bought me a couple of drinks and that's when I met Desmond – quite a nice boy I thought.'

'And what of the other man?'

'Other man? There was no other man.'

Bartlett was growing irritated. This woman had already interfered with this investigation and had been covert all along – and he was now having to bear the brunt of Greet's irritation.

'Sheila, we have more than one witness who says that you turned up with another man before you had even seen the Cooks. Who is he, Sheila?'

'Well, there was a man – but I don't know anything about 'im. I was just sitting 'aving a drink when 'e turned up and started talking to me. I didn't much like 'im and that's when I spotted Donald and I went over to 'im.'

'And what of the man?'

'Well, 'e followed me and pretended we were together.'

'What was this man's name?'

'I'm not sure – I don't think 'e said and I wasn't keen to make conversation so I didn't ask – I just wanted 'im to go away.'

'We've been told that you left the pub with this man – you were seen together.'

'Well, I didn't ... I think 'e left the same time an' 'e started following me but I gave 'im the slip and I didn't see 'im again.'

'What do you know about a ring, Sheila?'

'A ring? What do you mean – a ring?'

Bartlett was growing more impatient.

'Look, Sheila, I've got a feeling you're not being straight with us at all – I'll have to take you in if you keep this up ... you're being completely uncooperative and I don't know what you're hiding. You were seen in Bendix and Hall trying to sell an Egyptian ring. I want to know where you got it and where it is now.'

Sheila Parsons opened her small bag and pulled out the gold ring.

'OK, 'ere it is.'

She handed the ring to Bartlett.

'This is it? This is what all the fuss is about?'

Bartlett looked at the seemingly unremarkable ring then handed it to Boase.

'So?'

'So what?'

'Come on, Sheila – how did you get this? Who gave it to you?'

Sheila burst into tears. Boase offered her his handkerchief.

'Donald gave it to me. In the pub ... 'e said it was for all the trouble I'd gone to and for being such a nice friend to 'im on board the ship. But now 'e's gone and so's the other lovely young gent. Where can Donald be, Mr Bartlett? I didn't believe 'im – I even laughed when 'e said that things from Egyptian tombs were cursed and evil fell on those who interfered with them. I said there was no such thing as curses ... but now, well, it looks like poor Donald was right.'

Boase handed the ring back to Bartlett. The older man held it up in front of Sheila's face.

'See this? I'll keep it – looks like it's caused enough trouble already.'

'Oh! Mr Bartlett – I wish you would – I really don't care if I never see it again.'

Sheila was dabbing her reddened eyes with Boase's handkerchief.

'Boase, I need to speak to you – outside.'

The two men stepped outside the office.

'I can't arrest her, Boase. I haven't got anything.'

'Well, she's wasted a lot of time, sir. She's concealed information.'

'Yes, I know, but I don't think it's enough. I'm letting her go.'

'Sir, you can't – Greet will go mad.'

'I realise that – but it's my decision. I believe her somehow and, if I'm honest, I might be a little bit worried for her.'

'Worried, sir? Why?'

'Because, Donald was worried someone was trying to kill him, he had a really valuable – no, priceless – ring. Romanov was worried for him – and now I think I'm worried for her. Let her go,

Boase. But watch her – for her own sake.'

Boase knew Bartlett was usually right on things like this and he argued with the older man no further.

At seven o'clock Archie Boase was knocking at the Bartletts' front door. Irene opened it, accompanied by Topper who had barked loudly to inform that a caller had come.

'Archie. Hello – come in.'

'I'm sorry, Irene, I can't stop – my dinner will be on the table when I get back. I just wanted to look in and ask about this birthday party that your father mentioned.'

'Oh, yes. It's a girl I know from the St John Ambulance. You know I help out there once a month, well we met about six months ago. Her name's Jane Cornelius. She's ever so nice – she comes to help her mother. I think they're quite well off and her mother wanted to give a special party for her birthday at the house. They live in a big place out at the sea front. Anyway, I've ... *we've* been invited, if you'd like to come?'

'Irene, I'd love to come with you. Thank you. When is it?'

'Saturday – sorry it's a bit short notice. Would you call for me, say, at eight o'clock?'

'I'll be here. Thanks, Irene. I must dash.'

Boase put his arms around Irene and kissed her. He could stay like this for ever, he thought. Leaving her at the door, he made his way across the small front garden and out through the gate. He waved and Irene blew a kiss.

Sheila Parsons had thought that Falmouth had a really nice feel to it – much better than London she had decided. Now though, she was afraid. She wasn't too stupid not to realise that she might be in grave danger – but she could look after herself, she'd been doing so since she was fourteen. But she couldn't tell Jim how worried she was. She couldn't involve him – he was such a lovely man. No, he mustn't get mixed up in this. Well, it wasn't like she'd killed anyone was it? Nevertheless, there was someone who wouldn't hesitate to harm her and that person was always in the shadows. More than once she'd glanced behind her – just to be sure. Yes, she had to be sure if she was going to take care of herself.

The evening of the party arrived and Boase was early. He dawdled along the route to the Bartlett house but was still half an hour before he said he'd call. He knocked and waited. Caroline Bartlett came to the door.

'Hello, Archie, you're early.'

'Oh, I know, Mrs Bartlett – I'm so sorry.'

'Don't worry. Come in – I'm afraid you might have a little wait. And stop calling me Mrs Bartlett, it makes me feel about a hundred.'

'Sorry, Mrs Bartlett – oh, I mean, Caroline.'

'Come into the garden, Archie. Would you like some lemonade?'

'No, thank you.'

Boase fiddled with his cuffs, unaccustomed to evening dress, but he'd put up with it. He didn't want to let Irene down.

'She'll be down in a minute, Archie. She just

finished making herself a dress last night and thought the buttons were all wrong – she's just altering them.'

Boase sat and stroked Topper. He was so excited at the prospect of spending an evening with Irene.

Ten minutes later the door opened and there stood Irene. She wore a long dress of blue satin with a cream shawl and, of course, the golden bracelet given to her by Boase. She wore her hair up and fastened at the back with a blue comb. Boase stood up and walked to the garden door. He stepped inside.

'Well, do I look all right?'

Boase didn't speak.

'Archie?'

'Oh, yes, you look beautiful, Irene. Absolutely beautiful.'

'Well, let's go then, shall we? Bye, Mum – say good night to Dad when he comes in, will you?'

'Yes, good night, dear, good night, Archie – have a lovely time.'

Chapter Seven

Jane Cornelius hugged Irene on the doorstep and shook Boase's hand.

'Hello – I'm so pleased you came. There's loads of food and dancing, it's going to be such a lovely evening. Come in, both.'

The girl led the way through a very large hall,

passing an ornate staircase and the three continued until they reached an enormous orangery. Music was being played by a band from the Magnolia Club and a young woman was singing on a stage. Boase had never seen anything like this before – he thought there must be over a hundred guests here. A waiter came forward with a silver tray bearing drinks. Irene took one and Boase stared hard at the tray.

'Go on, Archie – it looks lovely, take one.'

Boase took a glass and sipped it. It was surprisingly nice.

'What would your father make of all this, Irene?'

Irene giggled and slipped her arm through Boase's.

'He'd absolutely hate it.'

'Yes, I think he would.'

The evening continued and Boase danced with Irene. He couldn't believe how lucky he was to be with the most beautiful girl in the world.

'Are you hungry, Archie? There's loads of food on those tables over there.'

'Only if you are, Irene.'

The pair went across to the tables. Boase looked puzzled.

'I'm not sure what all this is, Irene.'

'Nor me. Well, look – those look like something with cheese in, yes, look they're little pastry things. And here – what about one of these?'

Irene held out her hand to Boase. It contained one half of a hard-boiled egg with something curious filling the gap where the yolk should be. It was the something curious that worried Boase.

'Go on, Archie – look, I'll try one first.'
Irene bit into the egg.
'It's really nice – I don't know what's in it but it's delicious – go on.'
Boase took one, made a face, and put the egg into his mouth. He chewed and swallowed.
'Mmm – not bad. I might have another of those.'
'There you are, see – and you weren't going to try it.'
Irene reached up and kissed him on the cheek.
At about ten o'clock, Jane Cornelius came over to the couple.
'I say, you two have you met Alice and Sam?'
Alice Vyvyan and Sam Jackett were introduced.
'Alice does so much for mother with her jumble sales – I'm sure you and Irene have met before, Alice?'
'Yes, we have – nice to see you again, Irene.'
'Hello, Alice, hello, Sam.'
Jane indicated a door across the hall.
'Some of us thought we'd like to play a game. Will you join in?'
'Well ... what sort of game?'
Boase felt uncomfortable.
'We're going to play Memory Tray. It's so funny; we have a tray of objects and someone has to look at them and then it's taken away and one of the items removed. When it returns, you have to guess what's missing. Oh, come on – you'll love it.'
'Yes, let's, Archie – you should be good at that, you're always solving mysteries.'
Boase couldn't see the harm and so he accompanied Irene into a side room where there was a large table in the centre and several chairs placed

about. About twelve people came into the room to play. In the orangery, the music continued and the sounds of laughter and singing rang through the house. As one guest prepared the tray ready for the game, loud shouting could be heard from the front hall.

'Please let me come in – I've been invited. Yes, but I've lost me invitation.'

A woman's voice could plainly be heard – and one which sounded familiar to Boase.

Irene tugged Boase's sleeve.

'What's happening, Archie?'

'I don't know.'

Boase stood and went out into the front hall. A young woman was remonstrating with the butler who was refusing admittance. That woman was Sheila Parsons. Boase approached them.

'Sheila? What are you doing here?'

'Well, look who it is.'

Sheila Parsons was clearly glad to see a friendly face. Hearing the disruption, the hostess came to see what the noise was about. The butler spoke.

'Miss, this young lady quite clearly does not have an invitation to your birthday party...'

'Archie, do you know this girl?'

'Yes, well, sort of.'

'Well, in that case, miss – why don't you stay for the rest of the party?'

'Thank you, I'm much obliged. Thank you.'

Boase thought how kind Jane Cornelius was – it wasn't surprising that she got along with Irene, they seemed very similar.

'Well, we're just about to play a game – why don't you join us?'

'Well, I don't know as I'm very good at games, Miss...'

'Nonsense, we'll show you what to do – it's easy, and such fun.'

The group returned to the room where the other guests were seated, and the tray awaited them.

Two rounds of Memory Tray were played with great hilarity. Boase won immediately and was rewarded with a packet of cigarettes, which, since he didn't smoke, he handed to Sheila Parsons. The tray was prepared for the next round, the linen napkin placed on top of the objects. Sam Jackett took his seat in front of the tray, and the cloth was removed. He studied the items hard. The tray was removed from the room and the young man sat quietly with his eyes closed trying to remember.

Everyone in the room was shouting out the names of the objects in an attempt to aid the young man in his bid to win the cigarettes. Presently, the tray was returned and laid on the dining table. The cloth was removed. At once, there were gasps around the room. Irene screamed and another girl collapsed onto the floor. An object had been removed but another was in its place. Boase stood up and walked to the table. He looked at the tray. There, right in the middle of the objects, was a dismembered finger.

Bartlett lit his pipe.

'That was some business last night, Boase. Maybe you could tell me more of what went on now – I know that Irene was in a terrible state when you brought her home ... she hasn't slept all night.'

'Well, sir. As soon as I realised what happened, I sent for the police so that they could keep everyone in the house – as you know, they're still interviewing everyone. I've just come here to collect you so we can go over to the house and go through the place. I really don't understand it, sir.'

'Well, you did right to bring Sheila Parsons in – it seems that everywhere that woman is there's trouble. I've just spoken to her. She reckons someone was chasing her along the sea front last night and she just ran up to the house because she heard the racket and saw people in the front garden so thought it was the safest thing to do. When you recognised her and the hostess invited her to stay for the evening, she thought she was safe. But, she can't explain about the finger and maintains it can't be anything to do with her. What we do know is that she's a complete liar and can't be trusted on anything. You can bet your boots that she's more involved in this Cook business than she's letting on.'

Boase thought for a moment.

'Well, she could have been chancing her luck – just heard the party and tried to get in. You've only got her word that she was being chased ... although – that might not be as mad as it sounds, sir. Do you remember me telling you I saw Sheila Parsons in Killigrew Street?'

'Yes, I do.'

'There was a man waiting on the corner of Albany Road – and I thought afterwards that he looked like the man who was loitering outside here.'

'So, what are you trying to say?'
'Well, maybe he's following her.'
'Maybe he's following you.' Bartlett grinned for the first time in days.
'I don't know. Greet's arranged to have the finger examined ... he's really angry, sir.'
'Yes, Boase – now you're stating the obvious. He wants us off the case and I don't blame him. He's just been in here with a face like a funeral. What could I say?'
'Well, sir, let's go. Sheila seems happy to be in the cell – she's convinced she's in danger so why won't she tell us what's going on?'
'She'll have to now – we'll have another go when we come back.'
The two men left the police station and drove to the Cornelius house.

Jane Cornelius sat holding her mother's hand.
'Oh, Inspector Bartlett, this is such a shocking business. I don't know who could have done such a terrible thing.'
Mrs Cornelius dabbed her eyes with a handkerchief.
'Well, it looks like everyone who was here was spoken to last night and this morning and not one of them is likely to be a suspect. Are you sure no one else could have got into the house?'
'I'm sure. Since I've been a widow my brother has been very kind – he's made sure the house is very secure and we have several staff living here too. They were all on duty last night and it would be impossible for anyone to enter unseen.'
'Thank you, Mrs Cornelius – I'm sorry this is

so burdensome for you. Jane – tell me more about taking the Memory Tray outside. What happened when it was taken from the room to remove an object?'

'The tray was taken outside into the small hall and the person with the tray would remove an object and probably put it into their pocket, wait a few moments and then return it to the room. That's all really.'

'So, did you take it out yourself?'

'Yes, I was the first to take it out. I did just as I have explained to you.'

'Was there anyone watching you?'

'No, I don't think so. Everyone who wasn't playing was in the orangery – you can just about see the small hall from one end of the orangery but no, no one was near the room we were in.'

'Was it well lit in the hall?'

'Not really. There was no need. There was just a dim lamp on another table – we didn't need much light just there.'

'Well, can you show me where this happened, Jane?'

'Of course.'

Jane led Bartlett and Boase into the small hall and showed them the two tables. One where the tray was placed during the game and the other across the hall with a small lamp on it. Boase looked around the hall. It looked very different with the sunlight streaming through the little window at the end. He looked behind him and could just see the orangery at the other side of the house. There was a small staircase next to the little window. Boase walked over to it. There was a door under the stairs.

'Um ... would you mind if I open this, Jane?'

'No, please do.'

Boase opened the door. There was nothing inside, just one small wooden shelf. He closed it again and returned to Bartlett.

'I don't think we need to hold you up any longer, Jane. I'll just say goodbye to your mother then we'll be off.'

Bartlett and Boase walked across the road and stood watching the sea. The air was warm and several people were bathing. Boase pulled a paper bag from his coat pocket and opened it to reveal two slices of fruit cake. He offered the bag to Bartlett.

'Piece of cake, sir?'

'No, thank you, Boase. We should get back now. We must get something from Sheila Parsons.'

The two men reached the police station and went into their shared office.

'Get Sheila up here, Boase – and we're not taking any nonsense this time.'

Sheila Parsons was brought into the office and Penhaligon gave her a cup of tea.

Bartlett pulled out a chair.

'Sit down, Sheila. Look, we can't keep messing around like this – at least one man has been murdered and possibly two. Come on now. Tell us what you know – you're involved somehow and you need to tell us.'

'All right – I'll tell you what I know but you need to 'elp me. I think that, since Donald gave me that ring, my life 'as bin in danger. It's like this, see, there's a man – the one that was following me when I left the pub. It looks like 'e knew I 'ad the ring, well, you 'ave now, but 'e was very interested when 'e 'eard Donald and Desmond talking about it – and about Egypt.'

'We were told that you tried to sell the ring to Mr Bosustow, the jeweller at Bendix and Hall.'

'All right – yes, I did. I needed money – but, more than that, I thought if I got rid of it then I'd be safe. Jim said 'e'd take care of me and I didn't want 'im to get in trouble just cos of me. I don't want nothing to 'appen to 'im, 'e's such a luvly man.'

Boase stood up.

'So, who is this man? Describe him.'

''E's about thirty, with greasy black 'air – and 'e's got a gold tooth.'

'Is he tall? Short?'

'Not tall, no, about five feet five.'

'Was he following you in Killigrew Street the other day?'

''E might 'ave bin – I'm very frightened that 'e'll kill me just to get the ring. And I 'aven't even got it now – you 'ave.'

Bartlett asked Penhaligon for more tea.

'Look, Sheila, what happened last night at the party? Did you have something to do with that?'

'Oh, no. Of course I didn't. I couldn't believe what 'appened. It was terrible. I was as shocked as anyone – Mr Boase will tell you.'

'Right. Well, I'm going to get you a spot of lunch and then we'll start again right from the beginning – and you will tell us everything.'

By six o'clock that evening, Bartlett and Boase had really got no further forward with Sheila Parsons and still had no good reason to detain her further. She was free to leave. Bartlett slipped on his coat and handed Boase his.

'Well, my boy. I think we've done enough here. But, I want someone to keep a close eye on that young woman. Yes, you arrange that – she's still not in the clear with me, not by a long shot. But, not only do I want to know what's she's up to, I'm also rather worried for her. This man that's sniffing about – I really want to meet up with him. I don't like the sound of him one bit. Come on, I don't offer very often – let's have a drink in the Seven Stars.'

Boase thought Bartlett must be feeling very out of sorts to offer this – he didn't even like drinking in public houses.

'All right, sir – if you like.'

The two made their way down the road to the Seven Stars which was situated a two minute walk away from the police station. Stepping inside, they made their way to the bar. The barman came over.

'What can I get for you two gents?'

'Two pints of your strongest beer, please.'

The barman pulled the first pint and placed it on the bar in front of Bartlett who stared at it for a moment.

'Bit of a collar on it, isn't there?'

Boase grinned.

'I'll have that one, sir – you have the next.'

The second pint was delivered to the bar.

'That's one and two, please.'

Bartlett put the money on the counter and the

two found a seat. They sipped the beer and Bartlett scowled.

'Don't think much of this.'

'Oh, it's not that bad, sir. Go on, drink up.'

Bartlett continued with the beer but couldn't disguise the fact that it was nowhere near as good as his beloved Leonard's London.

'I shall be taking a couple of bottles of Leonard's home with me – can't understand why they don't sell it here on the bar.'

'Maybe they don't think it'd be popular, sir.'

Bartlett grunted.

'Tell me where we're up to then, Boase.'

'Well, sir, let's go over from the beginning, shall we?' Boase drew a small notebook from his pocket and then, digging deeper, pulled out a minuscule pencil.

'OK. One head, one body – not connected...'

'You being funny, Boase?'

'What, sir? Oh, yes, I see. No, not being funny. One head, one body. One coveted Egyptian ring – no, *priceless* Egyptian ring. Sheila Parsons apparently at the centre of everything, always like a bad penny but not enough to accuse her of anything. Do you really believe that anyone would give her a priceless ring – just for being nice?'

'Yes. If Donald thought he was going to be killed for it, he probably thought that was too high a price to pay.'

Boase licked the end of the pencil and where Sheila Parsons' name was at the top of the page, he wrote *'slippery'*.

Bartlett watched.

'Oh yes, she's slippery all right – beginning to

think she's too clever for us ... but she's involved, mark me, I just can't figure out how.'

Boase continued.

'Charlie Wentworth and that Romanov oddball. What about them, sir?'

I'm not sure ... Romanov said that Donald Cook was worried – no, frightened that someone was going to kill him. But, he couldn't say any more, although he didn't seem surprised when Donald disappeared. Go on, Boase.'

'Jim Penfold. We don't know much about him – or, come to that, how much he knows about Sheila. And, more importantly, we don't know why someone deposited the little gift up in one of his spare bedrooms.'

'No, I can't fathom that either.'

'Right, Boase. We need a better plan. This is what we do next.'

At ten minutes to seven Bartlett and Boase left the Seven Stars and headed for home.

Chapter Eight

Daniel Slade opened his hut on the Prince of Wales pier at nine o'clock as usual. As he stood his advertising boards against the side of the hut, a small queue had already formed outside. Irene had decided to treat her mother to a mystery trip. The charabanc was waiting and the warm summer day had brought several people, excited to be going to – well, no one knew where. The mystery trips were popular amongst older couples and groups of women and, being reasonably affordable, they were always well-subscribed. Daniel Slade's father had started the business and the idea several years before but with a horse-drawn carriage. Irene stood with her mother near the front of the queue. Suddenly, Elsie Treloar pushed forward and poked her head through the hatch in the side of the hut.

'Where are you going today, Mr Slade?'

'Good morning, Mrs Treloar. I can't tell you that, now, can I? If I told you then it wouldn't be a mystery – would it?'

'Is it Mevagissey?'

'Mrs Treloar, please. Would you like to buy a ticket for the trip?'

'Me and Mrs Bishop 'ave bin to Mevagissey twice and we don't want to go again. Is it Mevagissey?'

To the annoyance of everyone in the queue, Mrs Treloar persisted.

'If it's Mevagissey, I'm not goin' and nor is Mrs Bishop.'

'Please calm yourself, Mrs Treloar. As I've said, I can't tell you where we're goin' today.'

At that, Mrs Treloar barged her way back through the queue of people waiting to board the charabanc. She looked at Caroline Bartlett.

'I wouldn't bother, dear. It's Mevagissey. Me an' Mrs Bishop 'ave bin twice. It's not that good. We'll go somewhere else. Mr Pike is taking *'is* mystery trip to Portreath. I fancy Portreath – so does Mrs Bishop. Bye all.'

Irene giggled.

'Oh, Mum. Do you mind going to Mevagissey – we *have* been before?'

'I don't mind, dear. It'll be lovely just to see something different and it's going to be such a beautiful day.'

The two remained in the now somewhat diminished queue, bound for Mevagissey.

Quentin Bosustow surveyed the small, greasy man with the gold tooth. He tried to hurry his customer along – that man looked like he was about to steal something and he wasn't the usual type to frequent a high-class jewellery establishment such as this.

'Mrs deVere, I can assure you that this watch is of the finest quality – I'm absolutely sure your husband will be delighted with this as a birthday gift.'

Mrs deVere wasn't sure.

'Yes, Mr Bosustow, it's certainly a beautiful watch – but my husband is so very particular, you see. Let me see it again – now, you understand that it's the chain I'm unsure of.'

'Yes, you have said so, Mrs deVere, and I have explained that you can choose a different watch chain if you so desire.'

'Yes, yes, you're very kind. Did I tell you, Mr Bosustow that my husband had had the same watch for over forty years? Yes, a beautiful watch which had belonged to his father. Did I tell you what happened to it?'

Quentin Bosustow was still watching the man who was now in the corner looking at a case of rings.

'Mr Bosustow ... are you listening?'

The jeweller regained himself.

'Of course, Mrs deVere. What was that? Forty years you say? My, yes, that is a long time.'

'Well, do you know the Trawlerman broke into our house – we have a little place over at Flushing you know – and he took several of my beautiful rings along with my husband's precious watch. Now, you see, I don't think this watch you're showing me is quite the same good quality.'

'Well, I'm very sorry, Mrs deVere – you have looked at many watches now and I can assure you that your husband would be the envy of all his friends were he to own this.'

'Well, do you know, Mr Bosustow – it's three weeks until Mr deVere's birthday. I'm going to think about it. I'll call back perhaps next week. Would that be all right?'

'Yes, Mrs deVere. Perfectly.'

The woman left the shop and Quentin Bosustow was alone with the man.

'Can I help you, sir?'

The customer approached the counter and the jeweller drew back slightly.

'Yeah. You buy stuff, don't you?'

'On occasion, yes, I do.'

'You bought an Egyptian ring lately?'

'Well, no, as a matter of fact, no, I haven't – not that it's any business of yours. Was there something else I can help you with?'

'No, ta.'

And the man was gone.

Quentin Bosustow ran to the door, locked it and turned the sign to 'Closed.' He went into the back hall and telephoned to the police station, explaining what had just happened.

'What I can't understand, Boase, is how, in a place the size of Falmouth, we're letting people slip through our grasp.'

'Well, we caught up with Sheila, sir – she hadn't gone far.'

'I'm thinking more of whoever committed this terrible crime ... she has something to do with that but she's not saying. There's no way she actually did it, she's not capable. I bet she knows who did. If she would just talk to us...'

The desk sergeant knocked on the door.

'Sorry to interrupt, sir, Quentin Bosustow is on the telephone – you know, the jeweller from Bendix and Hall? Well, 'e's in a right state, says 'e must speak to you urgently, sir.'

'Right – coming.'

Bartlett went out to the telephone.

'Mr Bosustow, yes, how are you? What? Are you sure? Well, what did he look like? Just a minute. Short, dark, greasy hair – oh, right, a gold tooth you say? Thank you very much Mr Bosustow. Yes, thank you. Good bye, sir.'

Bartlett went back into his office.

'Boase, I don't believe it – that man who's been hanging round Sheila Parsons has just been into Bendix and Hall asking about the ring. He's still in the town.'

'Would you stay if you had anything to do with this, sir?'

'No, I wouldn't but he's not me. We've got to find him, Boase. This may be the lead we've been looking for.'

Several days passed and there had been no more sightings of the man with the gold tooth. Bartlett made sure he kept an eye on Sheila Parsons. He was genuinely worried for her safety and couldn't afford to make the situation any worse – another murder and the repercussions from Greet would be unthinkable. Not only that, Bartlett liked Sheila in a strange sort of way and didn't want to see her come to harm.

The platform at Falmouth railway station was crowded. Many people were taking advantage of the fine weather to get a little sea air and to enjoy the sunshine. A door at the far end of the waiting train opened and a passenger stepped down onto the platform. The short, dark-haired traveller looked around him and made his way to the exit, being stared at as he went. Handing his ticket at the gate he walked out onto the road and hailed a taxi. After a five-minute trip, the motor car stopped outside the Falmouth police station. The man paid his fare and, picking up a small bag opened the door of the car and alighted. He stood on the pavement staring up at the police station. Adjusting his hat, he walked up to the door and entered. As he walked into the lobby, Ernest Penhaligon stood up from behind the front desk. He stared.

'Can I help you, sir?'

'Yes, you may. My name is Leon Josef Nikolai Alexei Romanov.'

'Oh.'

'I wish to see Mr Bartlett; is he available?'

'Just a moment, sir. I'll see.'

Penhaligon knocked on Bartlett's door and entered.

'Sir, there's a very strange man asking to see you.'

Bartlett looked over his glasses.

'Strange? What do you mean strange?'

'Well, sir ... just ... strange. With a foreign accent.'

'His name?'

'I'm, well, I'm not really sure, sir.'

Boase had been listening to this from his side of the office. He stood up and walked to the door. He opened it about two inches and peeped through. He could see the desk and the man waiting there with his back to Boase.

'Sir, that's Romanov.'

Penhaligon looked relieved.

'Yes, that's it – *Romanov.*'

'Well, send him in then, Penhaligon.'

Bartlett pushed his cup into his top desk drawer and Boase did the same with his.

Romanov entered and held his hand out, first to Bartlett and then to Boase.

'Well, sir, this is an unexpected pleasure. What brings you to Falmouth?'

'I am worried for my friend, Inspector. Donald and Desmond were very close and I am worried, very much, for Donald. He has been missing for so long and I am very afraid. I have brought you the letter he sent to me.'

Romanov handed the light blue envelope to Bartlett who scanned the contents.

'This has taken a long time to get to you, sir.'

'Yes, I telephoned to you as soon as I received it.'

'He doesn't give an address of where he's staying, just East London. Do you mind if I keep this, sir?'

'No, please do, if it may help you.'

'So, why have you come all this way today – not just to give me this?'

'Well, no. I have come to see if I can help you to find Donald. He must be nearby somewhere, must not he?'

'Well, this is irregular – I don't see how you can help us to locate Donald.'

'My father has links to the Russian army – he has taught me everything I know. If Donald is nearby, then I will find him.'

'That's a strong statement, if you don't mind my saying so.'

'Well, whether you accept my help or not, I am staying here for a while – I have rooms at the Falmouth Hotel. I shall be visiting Desmond's parents tomorrow. They expect me. I am sorry to have troubled you.'

Bartlett stood up.

'Well, it's absolutely no bother but I'm afraid I cannot allow you to get involved in police work – or to hamper it in any way.'

'I shall not ... hamper you. Good day Inspector Bartlett. Constable Boase.'

Bartlett scratched his head.

'Well, what's he up to?'

'Dunno, sir – he's very odd, isn't he?'

'I'd say so.'

Boase couldn't sleep. He sat up in bed three times.

The third time he reached for his bedside torch. He looked at his watch. Ten past three. He got up, dressed and left the house through the kitchen door. He walked down Melvill Road and carried on towards the sea. Reaching Gyllyngvase Beach, he descended and jumped down onto the sand. It was a warm night and Boase took off his coat. He sat on a large rock and listened to the waves gently lapping close to his feet. He picked up his coat and looked through the pockets. He pulled out half of a small pork pie which he hadn't had time to finish the previous day. He felt hungry but had no appetite. He stuffed it back into the pocket and wondered why he didn't feel right. The business of the Cooks was getting him down – and he could tell that it was upsetting Bartlett too. Greet was making demands all the time, it was non-stop. But, these things didn't usually bother him. No. This was Irene. He couldn't sleep, he couldn't concentrate properly on anything and now, well, now – he couldn't even eat.

Taking the walk back up to the road, Boase resolved to do something about the situation he had found himself in. His money wasn't too bad. But could he give Irene everything she needed? What if it wasn't enough? What if he asked her to marry him and she said no? Boase shivered at the thought and walked back to the house.

The morning arrived soon enough and a weary Boase sat at his desk. It was eight o'clock. He yawned. Bartlett entered the office just at that moment.

'Careful, Boase – you could swallow your head doing that. How are you looking so tired this morning?'

'Didn't get much sleep, sir. Eventually I got up and went for a walk to the beach. Don't worry. I'm fine.'

'Penhaligon's just bringing some tea – that'll perk you up.'

Ernest Penhaligon brought two cups of tea and placed them on Bartlett's desk. He closed the door behind him. 'Sir, there's someone outside to see you.'

'At this hour, Penhaligon? Who is it?'

'Says 'is name is Canton, sir. 'E works out at the Cornelius place. Says 'e wants to talk to you about the night of the party, sir.'

'Well, send him in, Penhaligon.'

Bartlett threw a puzzled glance in Boase's direction.

Cardew Carlton, a tall, slim man of about forty, came through the door.

'Good morning, Mr Carlton. Well, what can we do for you?'

The man sat down in the chair next to Bartlett's desk and, drawing out a white handkerchief from his pocket, mopped his brow.

'I was at that party on that terrible evening, Inspector Bartlett, and I think I might be able to tell you something.'

'Go on. What do you want to say?'

'Well, sir, the thing is this. I was there that evening, serving drinks. I have worked for that family for over twenty years and I would do anything for them, they're such lovely people. I was so shocked by what happened, I can't begin to tell you.'

Boase wished the man would begin to tell something. He came forward and spoke.

'Please tell us. I remember you from the party – you did a very good job if I remember rightly.'

'Oh, thank you, sir, how very kind of you to say so. I don't normally serve drinks but Mr Robertson – that's the butler, had gone down with something and really wasn't up to serving and so I was asked to take his place for the evening. What I wanted to say was this; I came down into the hall this morning – from the top landing which emerges into the back hall and where the memory tray was laid during the game. Do you remember, Constable Boase?'

Boase nodded.

'I had just bent to tie my shoelace when I saw a couple of scratches on the skirting board. I pulled out my handkerchief to try to remove them – you see they just looked like dirt. Well, as I got down to the level of the floor, that's when I noticed.'

'Noticed what?' Bartlett and Boase spoke in unison.

'The small door at the rear of the hall is never used – and I mean never. Mrs Cornelius is very fussy about security and she never allows that door to be used. It would be quite useful at times but, no, she is most insistent. It is always firmly bolted. Today, however, the bolt was drawn back. That has never happened in my time at the house.'

Boase sat on the corner of Bartlett's desk and looked at the man.

'Do you mean that the back door was unlocked? That it could have been unlocked on the night of the party?'

'Yes, sir, I suppose I do – I only noticed it this morning so I have no idea how long it's been unlocked.'

'That's very helpful, Mr Carlton – thank you. We shall undoubtedly be paying another visit to the house ... just for another look. If you see anything else – anything unusual, please let us know won't you?'

'Yes, of course I will. I hope that this may have been of some help. Thank you. Good day gentlemen.'

Bartlett leaned against his chair and looked out of the window.

'You were messing about in the hall when we went to the house, Boase – didn't you notice the bolt?'

'No, sir – but then, I don't suppose I would have thought anything of it if I had noticed. So, it's perfectly possible for someone, using that unlocked door to have slipped in, put the finger on the tray and left again.'

'Well, I suppose so, but wasn't the tray minded all the time?'

'I assumed it was but I didn't go out there that evening. I played my turn at the game but that didn't involve leaving the room.'

'We need to have another look, my boy. Let's go now. If someone did use that door to come in then it's either someone who knows their way round or...'

'Or what, sir?'

'Or someone was let in by a person already inside.'

An oppressive and thundery late summer storm was brewing up as Bartlett and Boase headed for the sea front and to the Cornelius house. The door was answered by the butler.

'Is Mrs Cornelius in, please?'

'I'm sorry sir, Mrs Cornelius is out. Her daughter is here if she can help you?'

Bartlett removed his hat and stepped inside.

'Yes, thank you, that would help. Please tell her Inspector Bartlett and Constable Boase would like to see her.'

A minute later, Jane appeared in the hall. She was dressed in riding clothes.

'Hello, Jane. I'm sorry – are you about to go out?'

'Well, yes, but I've got ten minutes to spare.'

'I'm so sorry to bother you again like this but Archie and I would like to have another look in the back hall by the small staircase – if you don't mind?'

'No, of course not. If that's all you want then is it all right if I leave? You don't need me?'

'If that's all right with you then you cut along. I don't wish to delay you any further. We will only be a few minutes. Have a pleasant ride.'

'Thank you – Robertson will show you out when you've finished. Bye.'

Bartlett and Boase headed to the back of the house and the rear hall with the small staircase. Bartlett looked at the door.

'Well, it's bolted firmly now – that must have

been Carlton. So, Boase, what we have to imagine then, is that someone came in through this door – or was let in through it, had enough time to put the finger on the memory tray and then leave again. That's a bit much to believe, isn't it?'

Boase was looking at the floor near the stairs.

'What's harder to believe, sir, is that no one saw anything. It's impossible. We must have it all wrong.' The small hall suddenly went very dark and then brightened again as it was illuminated by a tremendous flash of lightning. A huge clap of thunder followed, bellowing over the house. Bartlett was staring at the frosted glass in the rear door.

'Did you see that, Boase?'

'No, what, sir?'

'Someone's out there – by the door ... quick, open it!'

Boase withdrew the bolt and pulled on the doorknob. Nothing happened.

'Quickly, Boase – open it.'

'Can't, sir, it's been locked with a key.'

'Then go out and run round the back as fast as you can.'

Boase left by the front door almost knocking Robertson to the floor, the butler having come to offer them some tea. He ran round the side of the house and stopped at the corner. The house being L-shaped, he could see across the lawn to the small hall door. There was no one there. He walked on into the garden. Nothing. He crossed to the hall door and knocked.

'That you, Boase?'

'Yes, sir – no one here.'

'Right, I'll meet you at the front of the house.'

The pair made their way back to the police station, dejected.

'Oh, I nearly forgot, my boy – Mrs Bartlett was wondering if you'd like to have supper with us tonight?'

'Are you sure that's all right, sir?'

'I wouldn't be asking if it wasn't – come over about half past seven?'

'Yes, thank you very much, sir. I will.'

Boase left the station that evening walking on air – soon he'd be sitting next to his favourite person in the whole world.

Caroline Bartlett answered Boase's knock at the door.

'Hello, Archie. Come in, you're just in time – supper will only be about five minutes, Irene's just putting out the plates. How are you keeping?'

'Oh, I'm very well, thanks, Mrs Bartlett – you?'

'Yes, I'm well too, but I wish you'd call me Caroline.'

Boase still thought calling her by her Christian name sounded too familiar but he would try to remember. Irene came out into the hall, closely followed by Topper who was licking his lips.

'Hello, Archie. I'm so pleased to see you.' Irene reached up and kissed Boase. He, in return stroked her cheek. Topper sighed and nudged Boase's hand.

'Oh, I'm sorry, Topper boy – I didn't say hello to you first. Here, let's have a hug.'

Boase bent down and put both arms around Topper's neck. Topper sighed again and returned to the kitchen.

'Archie, you're very silly with Topper. Come in and see Dad.'

Bartlett had a bottle of Leonard's ready for Boase and they each poured one into a glass.

'Come on, you two – no time for sitting around. Supper's ready.'

'Coming, princess.'

The two went into the dining room and sat down to a meal of cod, potatoes, and peas followed by a raspberry tart made by Irene. She glanced at Boase's empty pudding plate.

'Food all right, Archie?'

'It's more than all right – it's excellent. You're such a good cook, Irene.'

'Talking of cooks, my boy, who do you suppose was in the garden by the rear hall today?'

'I have no idea, sir, really I don't. If it was just a gardener or something then he would still be there when I got outside. No, it was definitely someone in a hurry who didn't want to be spotted.'

'Well, tomorrow we'll find out if the family was expecting anyone. We'll check the staff list too. Another beer?'

'Well, yes – I think I will, thank you. This Leonard's London is growing on me a bit.'

'And it's about time I should say. You've been drinking it nearly as long as I've known you. Cheers.'

All too soon the evening came to an end and Boase and Irene were once more on the small step at the front of the house.

'It's so nice to see you again, Irene. It's lovely to

spend time with you.'

'I've really enjoyed it too, Archie. I hope you'll come again soon?'

'I'd like that.'

Boase took Irene in his arms and kissed her and, as always, it was over too soon. He left her on the step and waved until he was half way up the road. He felt another sleepless night beckoned.

Chapter Nine

As Ernest Penhaligon came in with two cups of tea he closed the door behind him and spoke in a hushed voice.

''E's 'ere again, sir.'

'Who is?'

'That Rimanev ... you know, sir – the one from the other day. I mean Roomonev.' Penhaligon placed the two cups down on Bartlett's desk.

'I think you mean Romanov.' Boase chuckled.

'All right, all right – whatever 'is name is, 'e's 'ere.'

'I'll see him shortly. Tell him he'll have to wait five minutes.'

Penhaligon left.

'Oh, no – what does he want?' Bartlett sipped his tea and in unison both he and Boase put their cups into the top drawer of their desks and closed them.

Leon Romanov sat by the window and propped

his cane up against Bartlett's desk.

'Inspector Bartlett, I am a great admirer of the St John Ambulance.'

Bartlett stared at the man sitting opposite. This was still early in the morning and he didn't feel like playing games at this hour.

'Uh, is that supposed to have some sort of relevance?'

'Perhaps. I have an acquaintance through whom I gift money to the St John Ambulance.'

'Go on.'

'Her name is Mrs Agnes Cornelius.'

'You know Mrs Cornelius? How?'

'I have known her for several years through her good work and through my donations. I have money to spare and I like to put it to good use.'

Bartlett had no quarrel with that particular idea but he was worried about what was coming next.'

'Yesterday I had been taking tea with Mrs Cornelius – she had heard I was in the town and invited me. We have never met before and she wanted to thank me personally for what I have done in the past. When I was there I took the opportunity to have a look for clues relating to the party.'

'You did what? How did you know about all that?'

Bartlett was beginning to feel angry and undermined.

'Don't get upset, Inspector Bartlett. I may have information which could help you.'

'Such as?'

'Such as this.'

Romanov leaned forward and opened his hand.

He was holding a small tortoiseshell comb. Bartlett took it from him.

'What is this?'

'Well, you can see, Inspector. It's a comb.'

'Yes, I can see that. I mean, where did it come from?'

'I found it outside the back door of the small hall.'

'You!'

Bartlett leapt up from his chair, his face now very red.

'It was you that we saw at the house yesterday, snooping around in the garden. Why did you run off?'

'I didn't run off, Inspector. I found what I found and then I left the garden.'

'You have no business to be meddling in this case. If my boss found out about this, well ... I don't know what he'd do. You'd better leave.'

'I can assure you, Inspector, I am merely trying to find out what happened to my good friends, Donald and Desmond. You may keep the comb. Goodbye. Goodbye, Constable Boase.'

Romanov left.

'What a blasted cheek!'

'Calm down sir, you're getting too worked up.'

'You're right I'm getting worked up. How dare he interfere in police work to this extent! It's none of his damned business. Oh, I'm sorry, Boase. Take no notice. But he shouldn't be meddling in this. It's just making things worse.'

'Well, you know what they say sir?'

'What?'

'Too many cooks spoil the broth.'

'That supposed to be funny?'

'Well, yes, I suppose.'

'You're really childish sometimes, Boase.'

At that, Bartlett couldn't contain himself any longer. He laughed out loud. And he kept laughing. Boase started too until both were in fits of laughter causing Penhaligon to knock and come in. He looked startled.

'Yes, Penhaligon?'

Bartlett was mopping his eyes with his handkerchief.

'Sorry, sir. Superintendent Greet asked me to find out what all the noise was.'

Bartlett laughed again and Boase snorted.

'It's nothing, Penhaligon. Nothing at all.'

'Right-o, sir.'

The door was shut.

Bartlett and Boase looked at each other, somewhat relieved and feeling better for their uncommon outburst and lack of self-control.

'So. What of this comb then?'

Boase took the comb from Bartlett and looked hard at it, frowning and remembering.

'We've seen this before, sir. I'm sure. Do you remember?'

'No. Can't say I do.'

'Remember when Sheila Parsons first came here and she showed you her glove?'

'Yes.'

'I think when she pulled the glove from her pocket, this fell out – or one exactly like it.'

'No! Oh, not her again. So are we saying that she hid outside the back door and came in just in time to put the finger on the memory tray?'

'No, she was with us at the time of that particular game. But I noticed something else at the house, sir. I was going to talk to you about it this morning but then Romanov turned up.'

'What?'

'When we were examining the rear hall I looked inside the little cupboard under the stairs. That would make a good hiding place, wouldn't it?'

'It certainly would. Bit small though.'

'Well, it was empty. I couldn't fit in it but someone small could.'

'Like a woman?'

'Or a small man, I suppose, sir. But that doesn't make sense either. Sheila Parsons came in through the front door making a huge show of herself – just about everyone saw her. She wasn't in the back garden or the hall when we were playing the game. She stayed in the room with Irene and me all the time.'

'All the same, get her in again, Boase.'

Boase finished the cup of cold tea which was in his desk drawer and, grabbing his coat, went to the door. Just at that moment, the desk sergeant knocked and came in.

'Sorry to interrupt but I might have some good news for you both.'

Boase went back into the office.

'We could certainly do with some.'

The sergeant handed him an envelope and left. Bartlett tore it open and read the contents.

'That's very interesting.'

'What, sir?'

'The finger ... it had a scar on it. Look at this

diagram – it's a rather unusual scar. Yes, very distinctive. Time to find out if either of the Cooks had one like this, I think. But the park body had all its fingers, didn't it? How very helpful. Come on. Time to go. You get Sheila in and I'll try to speak to Dr Cook. See you back here later on.'

Sheila sat in the garden at Bar Terrace. Stephen had got the bicycle this time and Angela was bathing a doll in the fish pond.

'Angela, dear. Yer Dad'll be back any minute and 'e'll 'ave a right fit if 'e sees you upsetting 'is fish, make no mistake. Stop it now before 'e gets back.'

Angela threw the doll on the floor and scowled at Sheila.

'Da always lets me bathe Dora in the pond.'

'Well, it's almost time to go in for something to eat now anyway. I'm sure Dora is due a nap. Stephen, be a good boy and put the bike away now. Who fancies a sandwich?'

Sheila went into the kitchen. Hearing a knock at the front door she went into the front room and peered cautiously round the curtain. Inspector Bartlett said she should be very careful. There was no one there. Thinking it was the very badly behaved children who lived next door, she returned to the hall. As she passed the front door she saw a piece of paper on the mat. She bent down and picked it up. It was folded into four with no name on the front. She unfolded it and read:

I saw you at the police station. I want the ring.

I heard that young policeman talking to his boss outside.

He said you'd be safe now that they had it.
Get it back or you'll be sorry.

The note wasn't signed but Sheila knew exactly who had sent it. She hurried back to the front room and looked out again. She was surprised to see Boase standing on the step and ran to open the door, pushing the note under the large plant pot beside the hall window.

'Hello, Constable Boase. See, I 'aven't gone anywhere – just as you said. What brings you 'ere?'

'Inspector Bartlett would like me to take you to the station. He wants to speak to you.'

'Well, no. I can't. I can't leave Stephen and Angela on their own.'

At that moment, Jim Penfold came up the garden path. 'What's goin' on 'ere? Sheila?'

'Constable Boase wants me to go to the police station and I was just tellin' 'im that I can't leave the kids.'

'What now, Constable Boase? Haven't you pestered Sheila enough yet?'

'I'm very sorry, Mr Penfold but Inspector Bartlett has given me strict instructions to take Miss Parsons back with me.'

'I'm sure I won't be very long, Jim. I was just cutting some sandwiches. There's some fish paste if you want to finish it for me – the kids are starvin'.

'OK – but come straight back. You know Mr Bartlett told you not to be 'angin' round on yer own.'

'I promise, I'll come straight back.'

Sheila kissed Jim Penfold on the cheek and

went down the front garden with Boase.

George Bartlett walked up to Dr Cook's surgery. As he passed by a low hedge in the front garden he heard snipping sounds from the other side.

'Hello ... hello. Anyone in?'

Dr Cook emerged from behind the hedge.

'Good day, Mr Bartlett. I just had an hour or two to spare so I thought I'd tidy up this hedge – need to keep busy. Mr Rolling normally does the garden but he's getting a little old and rather unwell of late. I don't know how long he'll be able to continue with us.'

'He's doing a lovely job – I always admire your garden, Dr Cook.'

'Thank you. Ingrid is very fond of it.'

'I was hoping to have a quick word with you if I may?'

'Yes, of course. What can I do for you?'

'Did either your son or your nephew have a scar on one finger?'

'Why, yes. Donald did. There was a rather unfortunate incident when they were boys. They were playing, just over there actually, when a fight broke out. Desmond hit Donald on the hand with a metal spade. Did some irreparable damage too – he was lucky not to lose the finger. I think he's even been getting a touch of arthritis in it lately. It's quite a bad scar – Donald always wears a signet ring on that finger to try to hide it.'

Revisiting Bartlett's question, Dr Cook suddenly blanched and leaned back against a tree.

'Oh no, Inspector Bartlett. You've found Donald, haven't you? Please, you can tell me. I must know.'

'I'm sorry, Dr Cook. We haven't found your nephew. But we have reason to believe that Donald thought he was in danger and that someone was trying to kill him.'

'But *why?* Why would he think that?'

'That's what we're trying to discover – thank you, sir. We'll let you know what we find out at the very first opportunity.'

'But, Mr Bartlett – what about the scar? Why...'

Bartlett had left the garden and Dr Cook walked back into the house.

Sheila Parsons fidgeted in the seat.

'Come on now, Sheila – here's a nice cup of tea. Now, let's start at the beginning shall we?'

'I don't know nothing – no more than I already said.'

Bartlett sat next to her.

'Well, I think you do and you're going to tell us what you know. Right, first off – is this your comb?'

Sheila took the tortoiseshell comb and turned it over in her hand.

'Yes, it's one of 'em – I've got four. I wondered what happened to this. It's mine all right – look, I scratched a 'S' on the back. How did you get it?'

'You dropped it round the back of the Cornelius house on the night of the party.'

Sheila looked astounded.

'No, no I didn't – I wasn't even round the back of the 'ouse. Constable Boase will tell you. I never went there.'

'So, how did this comb, which you say belongs to you, come to be found by the back hall door at the Cornelius place?'

'I really don't know – 'onest I don't. I wasn't even wearing a comb in me 'air that night.'

'Sheila, that man who was hanging around – you said he was following you?'

'Yes, 'e was.'

'He's been seen around the town. He was asking in Bendix and Hall about the ring.'

Bartlett watched as Sheila grew pale.

'Has this man got something to do with the murder, Sheila? He's definitely keen to get this ring.'

Bartlett took a small key and unlocked a drawer in his desk. He took out the ring and held it up to Sheila. She drew back.

'I never want to see that again as long as I live.'

'Did Donald really give this to you, Sheila?'

'Yes.'

'Sheila. Tell the truth!'

'No. I stole it.'

'You stole this ring from Donald Cook?'

'No. I stole it from Desmond.'

'*What?* How did Desmond have the ring?'

'I think he took it. Donald was showing it to him in the pub and telling him how valuable it was. Donald told me when we were on the ship coming back to England that Desmond had always been jealous of 'im. 'E said Desmond was lazy and always thinking of the main chance.'

Boase put his hand on Sheila's shoulder.

'What do you mean, Sheila? Always thinking of the main chance?'

'Well, 'e said Desmond was always borrowing money – 'e 'ad no intention of finding a job, even with all them qualifications. The pair argued all the time when they was nippers. Desmond nearly cut off one of Donald's fingers when they was little. Seems 'e wasn't a very nice person. Always one for the ladies – but 'e just used them. Took them back to that little place 'e 'ad and then dumped them. 'E never wanted normal girls though, no, only rich ones. Donald said Desmond was carryin' on with a woman twice 'is age a few months ago – all cos she was rich. 'E 'ad to pack it in when 'er 'usband found out.'

'Sheila, do you know what we found in the house at Bar Terrace where you're living with Jim Penfold?'

'Yes. It's bin in the papers.'

'Then you know how serious this is. And that you could be in danger?'

'Yes.'

'Whoever it is that murdered Desmond Cook is probably responsible for the disappearance of Donald – and he'll stop at nothing to get this ring. That can be the only reason he's still around. Sheila, I'm keeping you here tonight – for your own good. I'll let Jim know. We'll be talking again in the morning. I'll get something for you to eat.'

'Oh, no, Inspector Bartlett. Please can't I go 'ome?'

'No, Sheila. I'm afraid you can't. I want you to think very hard tonight about anything else you've haven't told us already – I'm sure there's more.'

At five o'clock the desk sergeant and Penhaligon settled Sheila in for the night and gave her some food and a cup of tea. Penhaligon gave her a biscuit from his own tin and had a quick game of cards with her.

'I shouldn't be doing this, Miss.'

'It's ever so nice of you, Constable. Ta. And thanks for the biscuit. You'd better go now. I'll be all right.'

Bartlett grabbed Boase's sleeve just as the younger man was about to put on his coat and leave for home.

'Come back a minute, Boase. I haven't had a chance to tell you about the finger.'

'What about it, sir?'

'What Sheila told us earlier – it's true. Dr Cook told me that Donald was whacked on the hand with a metal spade by Desmond when they were kids – nearly severed it by all accounts. It's Donald's finger! And, listen to this, Donald always wore a signet ring on that finger to try to hide the scar.'

'So?'

'Think about it, Boase. Maybe the finger was cut off to get the ring – then it was discovered to be the wrong one?'

'Blimey. But that doesn't mean that Donald's dead though, does it, sir?'

'No. I don't suppose it does. But, that's what we need to find out – and sooner rather than later. If that's Donald's head, then there's not much chance of him being alive, is there?'

The heat of the late summer had brought storms in across the bay. To many the relief was welcome. Caroline Bartlett couldn't sleep. She sat up in bed and looked at the little clock. It was twenty past two. Bartlett woke immediately.

'What's wrong, princess? Can't you sleep?'

'I feel a little unwell, George. I think I'll just go down for a glass of water.'

'No you won't – you stay there if you're not well. I'll fetch it. What's wrong? How do you feel unwell?'

Caroline never wanted to worry her husband and this time was no exception.

'I think it's nothing, George. Really. I'll be fine in a minute or two.'

She held one hand on her chest as she spoke.

'This is your heart again, isn't it?'

'I don't think so. Maybe I just had a little too much to eat earlier on.'

'You barely ate anything. I'll get your water. Lie back on the pillows.'

Bartlett rearranged the bedclothes to make his wife comfortable and, slipping on his dressing gown, went downstairs to the kitchen. Topper was up on hearing footsteps on the stairs and he slowly wagged his stumpy tail as Bartlett descended into the hall.

'It's all right, Topper boy. Go back to sleep. Your mother's not very well and I've just come to get her some water. She'll be OK in a minute.'

Topper wasn't going to leave his master alone and followed him into the kitchen. Bartlett poured a glass of water and looked out into the garden. The storm was quite bad now and lightning was flashing across the kitchen followed by loud claps of thunder. Returning to the hall, Bartlett directed Topper to his bed and lay the dog's very own blanket across him.

'Go on – in you get. Don't worry. Good night, boy. Good night.'

The dog lay down and Bartlett returned to his room with the water.

'Here you are, princess. Have a sip of this.'

'Could you hand me my pills, George?'

'Still no better?'

Bartlett reached for the bottle of heart pills and, unscrewing the lid, shook one out into his hand and offered it to his wife.

'It's not so bad. I think I forgot to take my pills this morning. It's very silly of me.'

'You must try to remember, princess. I'd die if anything happened to you.'

'No you wouldn't, George. Besides – you couldn't, you've got Irene to look after.'

'I think Irene's got Boase, don't you?'

Caroline smiled, took the pill and handed the glass back to Bartlett. He placed it on the bedside table.

'Topper's worried about you too.'

'Bless him. He doesn't like the thunder much, does he?'

'Now you lie down and try to sleep. Wake me up if you're poorly again. Promise?'

'Yes, I promise. Stop worrying. It's very warm tonight.'

Bartlett pulled back the eiderdown and wrapped the sheet across his wife.

'Better, princess?'

'Yes, George. Thank you. Good night.'

Bartlett was now wide awake and lay thinking about the Cook case. Over and over in his mind went the people and the events. He was worried he was no closer and that wouldn't do. No, not one bit.

The clock on the parish church struck three times. Arthur Pouch couldn't sleep either. He turned over and over trying to find a cool place on the pillow. He thought he heard something in the garden. He listened. No nothing. Probably the tom cat after Polly again. He pushed back the covers but to no avail. Getting up he opened his bedroom window about two inches. The rain came straight in and soaked the windowsill. He closed it quickly. He felt very warm. He hated these thundery summer nights when he couldn't sleep. The little tabby cat, Polly, lay on the end of the bed, purring and watching Arthur's every move. She sat up and began to wash herself and then, jumping off the bed, made her way to the bedroom door. She looked up at the old man and miaowed twice and very loudly. He crossed the bedroom and, bending to stroke the cat, opened the door and went downstairs. Polly ran ahead in front of him and only stopped at the back door. It was opened and she went out into the rain. Arthur looked up at the sky and felt a bit cooler standing by the door. Maybe he'd have a little walk. Slowly he ascended the stairs and returned to the bedroom to dress. Back in the kitchen, he pulled down his mackintosh from behind the door and went out into the garden. Polly sat on the wall watching him.

As the old man reached the little lane at the top of his garden he heard a thud on the ground behind him. Just about to turn, he felt a searing pain at the back of his head as he fell.

Polly, who had witnessed the assault on her master, jumped down from her place on the wall and regarded the man lying in the mud. Arthur Pouch didn't move.

Chapter Ten

Benjamin Snow lifted the sack of coal onto his shoulder and carried it to the waiting cart. He was late this morning. He had hoped to start early today, for he'd promised to take Anne and Andrew, his six-year-old twins, to the beach to look in rock pools. Ben hated the heat and the beach but a promise was a promise – he couldn't undo it now. He hated, too, the number of times people had commented, 'You're called Snow – and you're a coalman?'

He wouldn't mind a shilling for every time he'd been poked fun at. He threw the last sack onto the cart. He stopped and lit his pipe, thinking. Why did people want a coal fire in the middle of summer? Yes, some people bought supplies now because of the generous summer discount, but others, mostly elderly, actually lit a fire every day of the year. Ah well, if they didn't, he'd have nothing to do.

Ben told Mary the carthorse to walk along the back lane to go out onto the street. He didn't ever lead her – she knew the familiar routes as well as the coalman did and all the customers knew her, often bringing out a carrot or an apple for her. He followed on behind, enjoying his pipe and the warm, damp summer morning and the fresher air the storm had left behind. As they almost reached the corner, Mary stopped and scraped the ground.

'Come on, Mary. Come on, what's wrong?'

Mary would go no further and scraped the ground harder and faster.

Ben walked from behind the cart and up to Mary's head. There was his friend, Arthur Pouch, lying on the ground. The coalman rushed to him and shook him.

'Arthur. Arthur. It's me – Ben. Arthur, wake up. What's 'appened to you? Arthur?'

There was no response and so Ben ran back down the lane and into the garden next door to his own, that of Henry and Eliza Hocking. Eliza was hanging some washing on the line. She looked up as she heard the gate rattle.

'Mornin' Ben – what's the rush?'

'Arthur Pouch 'as collapsed or something, in the lane – 'e's not movin' – come quick.'

Eliza ran up the back steps behind Ben Snow and together they hurried down the lane. Eliza, who had been a nurse in the war, knelt by the man on the ground. She poked and felt and listened.

'Well, 'e's still alive. We'd better get 'im inside – bring 'im to mine.'

The two carefully lifted Arthur Pouch onto the back of the coalcart and Mary skilfully managed to reverse back down the lane until she stopped outside the Hocking house. Henry Hocking had, by this time, come up to the back gate and he and Ben lifted the injured man down from the cart and carried him into the parlour. Eliza looked at him as he was laid on the couch.

''E's 'ad a bang on the 'ead. One of you 'ad better fetch a doctor – 'e don't look very good.'

Henry grabbed a jacket and ran as fast as he dared down Jacob's Ladder and onto the Moor in search of help.

Enrico Trewavas shook the doormat on the front step of the Star and Garter. As he looked up and down High Street, a short man who Enrico thought he recognised was walking up the hill towards him. As he waited to say good morning, the man disappeared down the slipway known as Barrack's Ope. Enrico, curious now, came out onto the street and walked towards the opening, stopping at its entrance. He saw the man descend and stop, as if to pick up something from the ground. No, he'd bent to strike a match on his shoe. Enrico watched as the man lit a cigarette and stood, motionless, looking out across the water. As the smoker turned round to return back to the street, Enrico ducked behind the building and went into the pub. He thought as he washed some glasses. Where had he seen him before? He swept the floor, puzzling over the man. That's it! He was the man with Sheila Parsons and the Cook boys. The same man Mr Bartlett was asking about. Enrico ran back out on to the street and, seeing the man in the distance heading towards the bottom of High Street, he followed and quickly came within yards of his subject. He held back and watched as the man paused to look in a small second-hand jewellery shop. Enrico, realising he was now conspicuous in his white apron, removed the offending item of clothing and, rolling it up, pushed it under his arm. Two people acknowledged him with: 'Morning, Mr Trewavas' and 'Nice day, Enrico.' The man barely noticed them. This might be a way to help Mr Bartlett, this surely is the man they're looking for.

After about ten minutes, the man reached the foot of Jacob's Ladder. Pausing to look behind him, he ascended the large flight of stone steps. Enrico, past his prime and rather overweight, never ventured up there. His body couldn't cope. He watched the man reach almost to the top and then disappear. Enrico was puzzled. If this man was wanted and was something to do with the murder, then why was he still in the town? That didn't make any sense. Enrico crossed the Moor and went up to the police station to see Inspector Bartlett or Constable Boase.

By now, well and truly out of breath, Enrico Trewavas entered the police station and sat on the bench seat in the lobby. He waited while a man was speaking to the desk sergeant.

'And your name is, sir?'

'Hocking. Henry Hocking.'

'And you found him outside in the back lane?'

'Yes, that's right. We managed to get a doctor to him and I think they've taken 'im to 'ospital but I thought I should report it to you. It wasn't an accident. Someone deliberately did this and my wife is worried. It's bad enough she's scared to go out after dark ever since that business in the park – but now, this.'

'Yes, Mr Hocking. I understand and you did the right thing telling us about it. I'll make sure someone looks into it.'

'Thank you. I 'ope you will. Goodbye, Sergeant.'

'Goodbye, sir.'

Enrico approached the desk.

'Good morning. Is Mr Bartlett in? Or Constable Boase?'

'Hello Mr Trewavas. How are you? Business good? Yes, they're both in ... did you want to see them? I'll just go and ask for you. Wait here please.'

A minute later, Enrico was being shown into Bartlett's office and relayed what had just happened.

'Is it any use to you, Mr Bartlett? It's definitely the same man who I saw with the Cooks and that young lady before.'

'You've done well, Enrico. Thank you. Thank you very much. Let us know if you hear anything else.'

'I will, Mr Bartlett. Always glad to be of help to you. Good bye.'

Immediately Enrico had left, the desk sergeant knocked and entered with two sheets of paper.

'Superintendent Greet would like you to deal with this, sir.'

He handed Bartlett the papers.

'What now?'

Bartlett scanned the information in front of him.

'But this is just an assault – probably a drunken

brawl. I haven't got time for this.'

'He was very insistent, sir.'

'All right. Thank you.'

Bartlett handed the papers to Boase who had been listening from his corner of the office. The younger man looked at them.

'This looks quite serious, sir. Arthur Pouch is in hospital. He's a very old man.'

'What? I didn't see that bit. Do you think it's something to do with him telling us about Sheila's acquaintance and the night at the pub?'

'I don't know, sir, but Mr Trewavas said he saw that man heading up Jacob's Ladder which is in the direction of Pouch's place earlier on. Could it all be linked in?'

'Right. You get up Jacob's Ladder now and I'll go up to the hospital and see if Arthur knows anything.'

'He might still be unconscious, sir.'

'But he might not. I'll see you back here later.'

The two men left and went in opposite directions.

Boase walked quickly up Jacob's Ladder enjoying the exercise. As he reached the top, he crossed into the small lane which ran along the back of the row of houses, including Arthur Pouch's. Reaching the old man's house, Boase stopped to look around. He walked along beside the garden wall and noticed some stones had fallen from the Cornish hedge. Boase thought it looked like someone had stood there and dislodged them. Then again, they may just have fallen out of place. He walked further along the lane and stopped, startled by what he saw at the very end. It was the man he had seen following Sheila Parsons at Killigrew. He was sitting on a wall, smoking a cigarette. Boase shouted out.

'Hey ... you! Stop. Stay where you are.'

The man looked up and, seeing Boase, ran along and out of the lane. Boase chased after him, almost knocking over a pram which had been left by the back gate for the baby to get some fresh air. He reached the end of the lane and looked up and down but the man had vanished. Boase ran up a small flight of stone steps and came out on Wellington Terrace. No one. He was furious with himself. How could he let him get away? Was that the man that attacked Arthur Pouch – but why would he come back here? None of it made sense.

Bartlett approached a nurse in the waiting area at the Killigrew Hospital.

'Excuse me, nurse, could I please see Arthur Pouch?'

'Well, I don't think so ... he's very unwell. The doctor says he's not to have any visitors. You're Inspector Bartlett, aren't you?'

'Yes, I am.'

'Well, the doctor certainly won't want you asking Mr Pouch any questions if that's what you're expecting.'

'I had rather hoped...'

'Well, I'm sorry, it's out of the question. You know he's mute, don't you?'

'Yes.'

'So he would have to indicate or write for you and there's certainly no chance that he would be capable of that.'

Seeing Bartlett's disappointment, the nurse softened.

'I'm sorry, Inspector Bartlett. Look, why don't you look in tomorrow if you've got time? He may be rather better then.'

'If that would be all right, then, yes. I'll look in tomorrow. Thank you, Nurse. Good bye.'

Bartlett replaced his hat and left the hospital.

Jane Cornelius held her mother's hand.

'Mummy, I'm sure whoever it was won't come back here again. Inspector Bartlett will find whoever has done all this.'

'But Jane, dear. I have felt safe in this house ever since your father died. I've so enjoyed living here but I really feel it's time to move on now. Maybe we could get a smaller place.'

'Mummy, you're really not thinking straight. All this business has been upsetting for you, I know, but you mustn't let this person win.'

'Jane, a vile murderer has been in our home. How else could that finger have appeared? *The finger of a dead man!*'

'Well, maybe, but you must try to put that behind you now, both of us must. Anyway, we don't know the man is dead. Whoever it was has no reason to come back. Please, Mummy, don't be hasty.'

'Whatever you say, dear, but my nerves really won't stand up to much more, really they won't.'

Jane took her mother out into the garden and they drank lemonade, sitting in the shade of the trees.

As the light faded, Jim Penfold sat on the garden wall and thought about Sheila. Why wouldn't the police let her go? What did they mean by 'it was for her own safety?' Sheila could never be involved in anything so terrible as murder. No, not Sheila. That was just nonsense. Walking back into the house he went upstairs and checked on Stephen and Angela. They were both fast asleep, Angela cuddled up to Dora and Stephen lying on a tin train. Jim went across to his bed and gently lifted the boy, carefully removing the train. He put it on the little table next to the bed and left, quietly shutting the door. He went to his own room, undressed, and got into bed. Five minutes later, feeling too warm, he removed his pyjama top and went across to the window. He pulled back the curtain slightly and raised the window a little way. Looking down onto Bar Terrace, he saw a young couple walking along hand in hand by his front wall. They stopped and the man lit two cigarettes and handed one to the girl. She kissed him on the cheek and, linking arms, they walked off in the direction of the town. Jim sat on the chair under the window. The air was a little cooler now. An old man was walking a small terrier on the opposite side of the road. The man was dragging the lead and the dog, having found something curious in the bushes, seemed reluctant to follow. The man tugged harder and the two continued their walk. As Jim was about to return to bed, his eye was drawn to the bushes in which the little dog had been so interested. The shrubbery there was quite dense but Jim was sure he could see a tiny light.

There it was again. Someone was in the bushes, smoking. He watched a moment longer then decided it was probably another young couple saying goodnight and he smiled to himself. Well, they weren't doing any harm. When he had courted his wife they found it so hard to be alone and everywhere they went his future mother-in-law accompanied them. Yes, he knew how they felt. Giving a final glance to the bushes, he got back into bed and was soon asleep.

Jim Penfold wasn't sure what woke him up. He didn't think he had been asleep for very long though. He lay in a daze thinking he should get up. Exactly what *had* woken him? Well, maybe he had had a dream – he was having too many of those lately, and they weren't good ones. Suddenly he heard a scream and a voice.

'Daddy. DADDY!'

Jim leapt out of his bed and ran to the door. As he opened it, smoke billowed through from the landing. He could hear Angela's voice more clearly now.

'Daddy. Daddy.'

'Stay there, Angela. I'm coming. Stay there.'

Jim ran back into his room and grabbing his previously discarded pyjama top, he wrapped it around his head and mouth, tying it at the back with the sleeves. He ran to the door again. He successfully reached Angela's bedroom. The girl was sitting inside the bottom of the wardrobe, sobbing. He ran to her and grabbed her to him. Back on the landing, holding his precious daughter, he could see the door to Stephen's room was ablaze. He paced back and forth, still holding Angela.

'Stephen. Stephen. Answer me. For God's sake. STEPHEN!'

There was no sound from the room. Jim pulled the pyjama top from his head and draped it over Angela. He ran down the stairs with her and to the front door. Withdrawing the bolts and turning the key in the lock, he reached the front garden. He sat Angela by the gate, well away from the house. Glancing up at Stephen's window he could see huge flames starting to burn the wooden frames. He ran back inside and upstairs again. He couldn't get near the bedroom door. He collapsed on the landing. Oh, no. Not Stephen. His precious son.

'Mr Penfold. Mr Penfold. Jim.'

Jim blinked and looked up. He didn't know where he was.

'Who are you?'

'I'm Nurse O'Malley. You've been in a fire but you're going to be fine.'

'My children. Stephen. Angela. I must see them.'

'You must rest now.'

'No. No, you don't understand. I must see them.'

The curtain was drawn around the bed and Nurse O'Malley was gone.

Bartlett lit his pipe. Using it as a spare finger, which he always did, he pointed at Boase.

'Get Sheila in here.'

Sheila Parsons was brought into the office.

'Sheila. Something terrible has happened and

I'm sorry to have to tell you.'

'Oh, Gawd. Wot's 'appened?'

'There was a serious fire at Jim's last night.'

Sheila screamed and fell back onto a chair.

'Oh, no. Are they all all right?'

'I don't think so. I'm sorry.'

'*All* of them ... all three?'

Sheila was sobbing and Boase handed her his tea.

'Drink this, Sheila. It'll make you feel better.'

Bartlett looked at her and couldn't help feeling sorry.

'Well, what we've heard this morning is that Jim is in hospital. He's very poorly and has some burns but he'll be OK. Angela was lucky that her father managed to get to her and bring her out ... it was her screams they think that alerted him.'

'And ... and ... Stephen?'

'I'm sorry, Sheila.'

Sheila let out a long wail and rocked backwards and forwards on the chair.

'No, please no, not Stephen. He's such a lovely little boy. No!'

'Look, Sheila, the firemen are there now going through the house. We've heard that the fire probably started near Stephen's bedroom door but we have to wait to find out. If that's true then Jim couldn't have stood a chance at getting inside the room to get Stephen out. I'm sorry to tell you such terrible news, truly sorry.'

Bartlett and Boase walked along to Bar Terrace. They couldn't believe what they were seeing. There was barely anything left of the top floor of the house. They walked along and into the front garden. Two firemen were sifting through some debris that had fallen from the windows.

'Excuse me. I'm Inspector Bartlett. Do you have any news of the boy?'

The two firemen looked at him and one spoke.

'Boy? No. What boy?'

'There was a boy asleep up in that bedroom last night. Didn't you find him?'

'No. We've still got a lot to do but I don't hold much hope of anyone coming out of that room alive.'

'Yes, all right, all right. But it's a small boy.'

Bartlett didn't much like this attitude. Boase just thought it must be the fireman's way of dealing with the things he saw regularly.

'I'm sorry, Inspector Bartlett. We've got lots of work to do here – you can see that. I can tell you that, so far, we haven't found anyone in the house.'

'Well be sure and let me know when you find him. And don't forget, we need to know as soon as possible if this looks like it was set deliberately.'

The fireman nodded and pointed to the front bedroom.

'Well, sir, it's not official yet so you didn't hear this. All the signs are pointing to the fire having been set deliberately up there.'

'What? Up there in the boy's bedroom?'

'Well, if that's his room. We found this by the door.'

The man picked up a petrol can and showed it to Bartlett.

'We need to investigate further, obviously, but this isn't the sort of thing you'd normally keep outside a child's bedroom.'

Chapter Eleven

Arthur Pouch was sitting in a chair beside his hospital bed. He slowly drank a cup of tea and looked out of the open window. He saw Bartlett coming across the lawn and stood up and waved. Bartlett, pleased to see the man up and about, waved back. Presently, Bartlett was knocking at the door and Arthur opened it to him.

'Good morning, Arthur. I'm so pleased to see you back on your feet. You feeling all right now?'

'Yes, thank you, Inspector Bartlett.'

At this Bartlett fell on to the bed and stared at the man.

'What did you just say?'

'I said, "yes, thank you, Inspector Bartlett".'

'Yes. I know. But ... how ... how did...?'

Arthur laughed.

'You're as astonished as I am. The doctor thinks the bang on the head has cured my condition – he says he's heard of it happening before.'

Bartlett stared.

'Well, I never – that's a miracle if I ever saw one. I couldn't be more pleased for you, Arthur, really I couldn't. Now I don't want to take advantage of your good fortune but I came here to ask you about what happened to you. What can you tell me?'

Arthur stared out of the window again and thought.

'I'm sorry, I don't really think I can tell you anything. I came out of the back garden gate and I heard someone jump down from the wall behind me and, well, that was all I know. The next thing I was in here. I'm so sorry. Do you know why anyone would do this to me, Inspector Bartlett?'

'I might, Arthur. But I can't be absolutely certain yet – but you can be sure of one thing ... I'm going to find out who it was. Yes indeed. Thank you, Arthur – and I'm so happy for you. Goodbye.'

'Goodbye, sir.'

'Irene's sent you a *billet-doux,* Boase.'

Bartlett pulled a small blue envelope from his pocket and pushed it across Boase's desk.

'For me?'

Boase tore open the envelope and read the contents.

'Did you know about this, sir? Irene has asked me if I'd like to come for lunch with you on Sunday.'

'Yes, she did say she'd like to see you. You coming?'

'If that's all right with Mrs Bartlett, then, yes, I'd love to. Oh, but that's tomorrow – I was going to come in here to do a bit extra.'

'Well, yes, but you've been working very hard – why don't you come in early then leave at twelve and come to the house. I'll be here so I'll leave with you.'

'Yes, thank you, sir. Thank you very much.'

Bartlett stood beside Boase's desk.

'Have we heard anything about Stephen Penfold yet?'

'Don't think so, sir– I'm hoping there'll be some news today. Doesn't look good though, does it?'

'No, I'm very much afraid it doesn't. I did have some good news this morning which you'll be very interested to hear.'

'Oh? What's that then?'

'I looked in on Arthur Pouch on my way here. You'll never believe this ... he can speak.'

'What do you mean – he can speak?'

'Just what I said. He said *"Yes, thank you, Inspector Bartlett,"* it's as true as I'm standing here.'

'Are you serious? I can't believe that.'

'It's true – I heard him with my own ears.'

'Well, good for him.'

'Yes, not good for us though – he couldn't tell me anything about his being attacked. He didn't see anything.'

'Don't be discouraged. We'll find out what's going on here soon. I've just got a feeling.'

Dinner at the Bartlett house was, for Boase, an exciting event as usual. He put on his decent shirt and second-best trousers and, glancing at himself in the hall mirror, went out through the front door and headed for Penmere Hill. As he lifted his hand to knock at the front door, Topper let out his usual 'it's a friend' bark. Boase could see Irene through the frosted glass and his heart leapt. She opened the door and stood there with Topper.

'Hello, Archie. Come in.'

'Thanks for inviting me, Irene. You look nice.'

Boase thought Irene looked different this evening – even more beautiful than usual, if that could be possible.

'Mum and Dad are in the garden – it's still so warm. We wouldn't have heard you if it wasn't for Topper.'

The two, together with Topper, walked through the house and out into the back garden where Bartlett and Caroline were sitting on a wooden bench.

'Good evening, Archie. I'm so pleased you could come.' Caroline stood up.

'Thank you for inviting me – please don't stand up.'

'I was just going in to pour you a cup of tea.'

Bartlett leaned forward and pulled a bottle of beer from underneath the bench.

'Boase doesn't want tea – here, Boase, have a bottle of Leonard's. Come on now, here's a glass.'

'Thank you very much, sir.'

Boase took the bottle and poured the contents into the glass.

'Cheers, all.'

Boase sat on the lawn next to Irene and Topper. The three of them looked at each other.

'Come on – you sit up here.'

Caroline got up from her place and walked across the lawn.

'George – help me with the plates, will you?'

'I was just about to tell Boase...'

'George!'

Bartlett considered himself told and rose from his seat, taking his precious beer with him. He followed Caroline into the kitchen.

'I just wanted to tell Boase about...'

'Yes, well I just want them to be alone. They don't spend much time together as it is and I'm sure when they do they don't want us looming over them. Don't you remember when we were trying to get rid of my mother, bless her? When we wanted to be alone together, George?'

'Well, yes. Anyway, stop that sort of talk now – they'll be in here in a minute.'

Caroline smiled at her husband. It always made her laugh how he felt embarrassed to display any affection in public and yet he was such a romantic at heart.

'Go and call them now, George, will you? Oh, no wait – look.'

Bartlett and Caroline looked out of the kitchen window and watched as Boase and Irene kissed on the bench. They both smiled.

'George, look at Topper.'

The pair laughed out loud as they saw Topper walk around the back of the bench until he was out of view of the lovers, sinking himself into the herbaceous border.

The four sat at the table in the dining room, Topper installing himself between the chairs of Bartlett and Boase, hopeful for the usual morsels that came his way.

'Mum and I had such a lovely day in Mevagissey last week, Archie.'

'Yes, I heard you were going. Looks like you had some nice weather.'

'It was ever so funny. Mrs Treloar and Mrs Bishop must go on every mystery trip – and they succeed in ruining it for everyone. Mrs Treloar barges straight to the front of the queue and asks where they're going, then she ends up having an argument with everyone.'

Bartlett snorted.

'I'm surprised they don't get banned from the trips.'

'Well, we didn't mind, did we Mum?'

'No, dear. It was a very nice day – I enjoyed it.'

'Talking of mysteries, I wish we could get a grip on this Cook business, Boase. Greet's beginning to get on my nerves. He's going to have us off the case very soon, Boase, mark my words.'

'I know, sir. I just wish we could get a break. I don't know how much more we can do. Something or someone's got to give soon.'

Irene felt sorry for Boase and patted his hand.

'Don't worry, Archie – I know you and Dad are giving it your all. It'll come together soon, I just know it.'

Both Bartlett and Boase, at that moment, wished for Irene's confidence.

At eleven o'clock, Boase said his goodbyes to the Bartletts, spending more time on the step with Irene than he usually did. He didn't want to leave. As he looked at her he could sense something different about her – just what he couldn't say. She was just so beautiful. He eventually tore himself away and headed for home, his head full of the girl he knew he wanted to marry.

Cardew Carlton stood at one end of the kitchen in the Cornelius house. Daisy Davies sat on a chair by the butler's pantry.

'Daisy – you must tell me what's going on. I came in here and you were stuffing food into your apron. Why, in only the last four weeks, large quantities of food have gone missing from this kitchen to say nothing of the drink. Poor Cook is having a fit because she doesn't like thievery – and neither do I. Come on, Daisy. What's going on?'

'I'm so sorry, Mr Carlton, really I am. I can't tell you what's bin goin' on – I want to, but I can't.'

'Daisy, you could lose your job over this and I won't be able to save you. The mistress and Jane searched high and low to find a little seamstress as good as you and you were all lucky to find each other. Not all Barnardo's girls get such a good chance as this. Tell me what's going on.'

'No.'

Daisy mopped the tears from her eyes.

'I've caused so much trouble, really I 'ave. I'll 'ave to leave anyway.'

'Well, it might not come to that if you tell the truth.'

'Yes it will.'

'I'm trying to help you, Daisy. Just admit you stole the food and make an arrangement to repay the cost. The mistress is a charitable and good woman – she won't put you out.'

'But she will, Mr Carlton. It's not just about the stealing.'

'What is it then?'

'Oh, no. I really can't tell you.'

'Daisy – you must. What can be so bad? I can help you. I don't want to see you go.'

'I think I left the back door unbolted.'

Daisy sobbed harder.

'*You?* Daisy, no one must use that door – you know that.'

'Yes. I do. I've been talking to Percy the butcher's boy and, well, I've been seein' 'im round in the back garden. I didn't ever leave the door but it's so quiet in the back 'all and we've just bin snatching a few minutes to talk from time to time. 'E wants to marry me, Mr Carlton.'

'Well, this is a turn-up for the books, my girl. Marry? But you're only sixteen.'

'Yes. Well, I love 'im and when I get put out of 'ere, I won't 'ave anyone else.'

'You're not ... in the family way, I hope? Is that what all this is about?'

'Oh, no, sir! No, nothing like that. Percy is a gentleman. But I 'ave bin very silly – and careless. We've bin 'aving a bit of fun, like I said. Well, one day I was just wavin' cheerio and as Percy left the garden a man ran up to me as I was about to shut the door and asked me for food and drink – an' some clothes. 'E said 'e knew about me an' Percy and if I didn't feed 'im then Percy would get badly 'urt an' I might never see 'im again. I haven't seen the man for a while but I've been taking a little bit o' food and keeping it under me bed in case 'e turns up again. 'E came a couple of times and I just left a little parcel outside the back door. The last time I saw 'im, 'e said 'e'd be back two days later. I told 'im 'e mustn't cos of the party an' all – 'e said 'e'd be 'ere anyway and I was to leave the food outside the door as usual.'

'Who was this man, Daisy?'

'I don't know 'is name.'

'Right, get your coat.'

'Where are you takin' me, Mr Carlton?'

'We're going to the police station and you're going to tell Inspector Bartlett everything you've just told me.'

'Am I in trouble, Mr Carlton?'

'Not if I can help it – but you should have told the truth, Daisy.'

The two left the house and walked to Berkeley Vale.

Bartlett was tapping his fingers on the desk. Boase was eating a ham sandwich and rifling through some papers.

'That's really annoying, sir.'

'What? Oh, sorry, Boase. I was miles away. What are you up to?'

'I'm just going through the postal delivery, sir. Quite a few things here for us both, mostly uninteresting. I'm just trying to get ahead with it all while I've got a minute or two. Hang on a minute.'

Boase put down his sandwich and brought an envelope over to Bartlett.

'Sorry, sir. This must have been delivered last night – missed it.'

'Well, it seems to me you've been a bit distracted lately, I can't think why that might be.'

Bartlett knew perfectly well why Boase couldn't concentrate.

'Anyway, isn't all this Penhaligon's job?'

'Well, yes, sir. Usually. But I gather his mother is very unwell at the moment and he's been allowed to take a couple of days off.'

'Is it serious? Greet isn't normally so amenable.'

'I think it might be, sir.'

'I'm sorry. Mrs Penhaligon is a very nice woman. I hope she'll be all right. Blimey, Boase. This letter is from the fire chief.'

'What's it say, sir?'

'Wait a minute.'

Bartlett lowered his glasses from their resting place on his forehead and read on.

'I can't understand this, Boase. It doesn't make sense.'

'What doesn't, sir?'

'Well, you know I was asking about the Penfold boy?'

'Yes, I was with you. They hadn't found his body by the time we got there.'

'They still haven't.'

'What do you mean, sir?'

'It says they've been right through the house and garden and they've found nothing. It goes on to say, too, that the fire was definitely started deliberately.'

Boase sat back down in is chair.

'Are you going to say this is to do with Sheila Parsons as well, sir?'

'I don't know. Bit of a coincidence, isn't it? If the man who's been hanging around had something to do with the fire, well ... maybe he set it hoping she'd be in the house?'

'But then he'd never get the ring, would he?'

'This is getting deeper by the day, Boase. Deeper by the day.'

As the two men pondered over the contents of the letter, the desk sergeant knocked at the door.

'Excuse me sir, Archie. There's a Mr Carlton outside wants to see you. Says it's urgent. He's got a young lady with him.'

'Send them in.'

Cardew Carlton, accompanied by Daisy, entered the office.

'Good afternoon, Mr Carlton. What can we do for you?'

'Good afternoon, Inspector Bartlett, Constable Boase. This is Daisy Davies – she's seamstress to the Cornelius family. Say hello, Daisy.'

Daisy said nothing but stood behind Mr Carlton.

'Something has happened at the house, Inspector, and I thought you ought to know about it in case it was relevant.'

'Well, why don't you both have a seat and talk to us?' Bartlett pulled a chair from under the window for Daisy and Boase offered his to Carlton.

'What do you want to tell us?'

'I think Daisy should explain, Inspector.'

Daisy nervously retold the story about Percy and the back door and the stranger threatening her.

'Daisy, Constable Boase and I are here to help, so please tell us everything you can. What did the man look like?'

'Well, I can remember him very plainly, sir. 'E was quite short, black 'air and an 'orrible gold tooth. He was very nasty looking.'

'And why did he want food?'

''E never said – just that 'e would turn up at a certain time and expect me to give 'im stuff. So I did cos I was afraid for Percy.'

'Did you let him into the house, Daisy?'

'No, sir. Never.'

'Do you remember leaving the bolt off the door?'

'I'm not sure. I really can't remember – 'e was upsetting me so much it's 'ard to remember. I'm very particular – I know the mistress doesn't like anyone using that door.'

'Right, thank you, both. Be sure to let us know if this man reappears or if you think of anything else, won't you?'

'Yes, we shall, Inspector. Good afternoon.'

The pair left and Bartlett and Boase looked at each other.

'Why can't we find him, sir? This is ridiculous – everyone seems to have bumped into him except us. He's very clever.'

'Well, he's not going to beat us. What's your take, Boase? Do you think he went to the house for food just to have a snoop round before the party? That would be risky especially since Daisy told him there'd be lots of people around.

'Dunno, sir. Looks like he hasn't been back there since– Anyway, I've been making a few notes.'

Bartlett smiled to himself. That's what he liked about Boase – methodical to a fault. The younger man flipped open a pad of paper and began to tell Bartlett what he had written.

'Well, sir, this is my theory. Could be all wrong, of course, but, in the absence of anything else...'

'I'm listening.'

'I think that maybe this man – let's call him, I dunno, Paul. Let's say Paul killed Donald Cook and Desmond Cook...'

Bartlett stared at Boase.

'So you think they're both dead too?'

'Please don't interrupt, sir. I'll lose my thread. Let's say they are – we have had two separate corpses after all, that much we know. If it's not both Cooks, then who? Paul wants the ring – desperately. He finds out that Sheila has it...'

'How?'

‘Sir, please. He finds out that Sheila has it and starts following her. We’ve seen him hanging around. He has a finger from the missing body – of which we don’t know the whereabouts, but it looks to be Donald.’

‘But she said she only went up to the house because he was following her – it wasn’t planned.’

‘Hmm. All right – I’ll give you that for now. What if he wasn’t actually following her that night – he was coming up to the house for the food parcel? So, he comes round the back of the house, looks for the food, and when it’s not there he enters through the rear door to see if it’s in the hall.’

Bartlett put down the reading spectacles he had been fiddling with and looked at Boase.

‘Really?’

‘Why not? Then he conceals himself in the little cupboard under the stairs ... maybe when he hears someone he has to hide ... perhaps when the tray comes out – now, remember where the table is that held the tray? It’s right by the cupboard. As long as the person with the tray isn’t looking, he can quickly open the door, put the finger on the tray and job done. We’ve been told it was quite dim in the hall that evening ... and I remember it was. I’d say that each person was given two minutes to memorise the contents of the tray.’

‘But that assumes that the person minding the tray wasn’t minding the tray – and that Paul was in the house at the same time as you.’

‘Yes I know. But how could I possibly expect anything like that, sir? Anyway, I can’t remember who took the tray, I can check – it was a man, but maybe he removed one of the items, put it into his pocket, then went to get a drink or something while he was waiting to return the tray. And there's another thing, sir. Paul knew that Sheila had come up to the house and if he did come into the rear hall he would have heard her.'

'What do you mean?'

'Well, sir, Irene was really laughing at Sheila – because she was so loud. She was shouting out the objects on the tray louder than anyone. I'm surprised they didn't hear her in Penryn. So anyone in the hall would know she was there – maybe that's why Paul put the finger on the tray; because he knew she was nearby and that it would incriminate her.'

Bartlett scratched his head.

'Come along, sir. Play the game – we have to try to fill in the gaps until we know.'

'Yes, I suppose so.'

'Anyway, next, Paul sets the fire at the house where he has previously concealed the head, thinking that Sheila Parsons is there that night – he couldn't know that she was here in a cell.'

'So, where's the boy Stephen?'

'Well, that's where I come unstuck. But you asked for my theory and that's it – so far.'

'Some of that makes sense, Boase. But there are a lot of gaps.'

'I know but we should be able to fill them in, shouldn't we?'

'We have to my boy – no two ways.'

Chapter Twelve

Topper sat under the breakfast table while Bartlett drank a cup of tea and ate two slices of bread and butter. The dog looked hopefully up at his master and gratefully and gently took a small piece of the bread which was handed to him.

'Well, Topper boy, I hope things look up today and that's a fact. Wish me luck old chap. Aren't you such a good boy – so loyal. I'd really miss you if you weren't around.'

The early morning silence of the dining room was shattered by shouting from upstairs.

'Dad, Dad – come up quickly.'

Bartlett ran into the hall and up the stairs, two at a time. Irene was in her parents' bedroom where her mother was slumped on the floor.

'Help me get her up, Dad. I think she's fainted.' Bartlett knelt to the floor and took his wife in his arms. He looked at her face.

'Princess, princess! Oh no! Princess. Please wake up. Irene, call someone – quickly.'

Irene ran back down the stairs not even knowing who to fetch.

Bartlett lay his wife on the bed, watching and listening. He could see her breathing.

'Princess. It's me – your George. Please speak to me.'

Caroline, hearing the voice, moved her head and opened her eyes.

'George, is that you?'

'Of course it's me, princess. Oh, you gave me such a fright. Would you like a sip of water? Here you are.'

He gently leaned across her and picked up a glass of water, offering it up to his wife's lips. She took a sip. He replaced the glass and held her hand. Slowly her colour returned.

'What happened, princess? Did you faint?'

'I think so. The room went dark suddenly and I had a pain.'

'Where? Where did you have a pain? Your heart?'

'Well, in my chest and my arm.'

'Irene's gone to get someone – she'll be back in a minute.'

'Yes, I just called her and she came running, God bless her.'

'Well, it's a good job you weren't on your own, that's all I can say. You really need to take things easier, my beautiful girl.'

Bartlett stroked his wife's hair.

'I do take things easy, George. I couldn't possibly do any less.'

'Yes you could – and you're going to have to.'

The two lay on the bed, Bartlett rocking Caroline in his arms. A tear fell from his cheek onto hers. He looked away. Topper stood on the landing looking into the room.

'It's all right, boy. She's all right. Look – you can come in.'

The dog wandered around to the side of the bed and looked at Caroline then returned to Bartlett and licked the man's hand reassuringly.

'She's OK, Topper boy. She's OK. Go down and

wait for Irene now. She'll be here in a minute.'

The dog obeyed and returned down the stairs and sat by the front door.

Boase looked at the clock. Ten past ten. He hoped Bartlett was all right – he was never late for work. More, he hoped nothing had happened to Irene. Now he was panicking. He made a cup of tea and asked the desk sergeant if he had heard anything. Just as they were speaking, Bartlett came through the front door of the station.

'Oh, good morning, sir. Everything all right?'

'Not really, Boase. Mrs Bartlett was taken ill this morning and I had to wait with her.'

'Nothing serious I hope, sir. Here's a cup of tea. Come in and sit down.'

'Well, I'm worried that it *is* serious. Mrs Bartlett has heart trouble, as you know – well, I've never seen her so bad as this morning. Fair shook me up it did.'

'Maybe you should have the day off, sir. I'm sure we can manage.'

'That's kind of you, my boy, but we've got far too much on – Irene's with her anyway. The doctor's been and she's a bit more settled now. He's given her some new medicine so she's going to try that. Thanks, Boase.'

'And Irene ... is Irene all right, sir?'

'Irene is fine. She was marvellous this morning – she's such a good girl, my Irene.'

'I know, sir.'

'Thanks for the tea, Boase. I needed one.'

'You're more than welcome. There's a letter here addressed to you – some kid delivered it this morning. Here you are.'

Boase slid a brown envelope across Bartlett's desk. The older man looked at the envelope.

'What's this – Topper's got better writing.'

Boase chuckled and watched as Bartlett opened the envelope.

'Oh my...'

'What is it, sir? Bad news?'

'I don't know what sort of news this is. Have a look.'

Bartlett handed the note to Boase who laid it on his desk and read it.

I've got the Penfold boy. If you want to see him alive then you have to give me the ring. It's mine and I want it. Sheila Parsons is a murderer and you want to watch her. I know she did them both. She'll probably strike again soon – she's evil all right. Just make sure I get the ring. I'll send another note with instructions tomorrow. You can tell the man Penfold that his boy is safe.

'He's got Stephen, sir. He's alive.'

'Well, he says so – how do we know? What do we do now?'

'Well, wait for the instructions, I suppose. We have to get the boy back. Are you going to tell Jim Penfold?'

'Well, I went up to the hospital last night and told him the boy hasn't been found. He's desperate. I might leave it until we know more what's happening. It could make things worse for him.'

'Right-oh, sir.'

Bartlett lit his pipe. He looked out of the window wondering how Caroline was. What would he do if anything happened to her? How could he live without her? His thoughts were interrupted by Boase.

'Do you want me to go up and tell Greet, sir? He needs to know what's happened.'

'Yes. Right – he does. Come one, we'll go up and see him together. Hang on to your hat.'

The two went up to the next floor to Superintendent Greet's office to relay their latest news.

At Penmere Hill, Caroline Bartlett was feeling a little better. She was sitting up in bed with a shawl wrapped around her shoulders. Topper lay on the rug beside the bed. He looked up as Irene came into the bedroom.

'I brought you some soup, Mum. Topper, what are you doing up here? Mum's not well.'

'Leave him, Irene – he's making me feel better. I'm really not hungry, dear. All that this morning has taken it out of me a bit.'

'I know – and that's why you need to eat something. Go on. Please try a little – before Dad comes home. He'll be so pleased to think you've eaten something.'

'Well, maybe just a small drop.'

Iren sat on the bottom of the bed and watched while her mother managed half a bowl of thin soup. She took the tray and the bowl back and placed them on the dressing table.

'Here, Mum. Let me do your pillows, you don't look very comfortable.'

'Thank you, dear. You're very good to me. You know I can manage on my own – I *could* manage on my own if you weren't here.'

‘I’m not going anywhere, Mum. Don’t worry.’

‘But I do worry, Irene. You can’t spend the rest of your life looking after me. What about Archie?’

‘What about Archie?’

Caroline took her daughter’s hand.

‘Irene, he’s very much in love with you. I wouldn’t be surprised if he asked you to marry him very soon.’

‘Mum! Don’t be silly.’

‘I’m serious – and so is Archie. Your father and I can tell and if ... when, he asks you, then you’ll have to think very seriously. We don’t want you wasting your life here with us.’

‘You trying to get rid of me, Mum?’

‘No – of course I’m not trying to get rid of you. I just want you to be happy. You do like Archie, don’t you.’

Irene stopped fiddling with the pillows and sat back down on the bed.

‘I really like him, Mum. A lot.’

‘Well then, don’t take a backward glance if you get a chance to make a life for yourself. I doubt you’d be far away anyway – Archie’s a Cornishman through and through, yes, very proud to be Cornish.’

‘Thanks, Mum. I’ll make you a cup of tea.’

Irene went down to the kitchen. She didn’t like the conversation she had just had. Her mother was worried that she’d die – yes, that was it. If she did, perish the thought, Irene would have to look after her father. Oh, what a turmoil. She felt a little sick and went out into the garden for some air. She couldn’t think about all this just now – it was all too much.

'What's the best way to catch him, Boase?'

Bartlett looked to his assistant for advice.

'Well, I think our best bet is to wait for another note.'

'But what if that doesn't happen?'

'Well, he wants the ring, doesn't he?'

'Yes, but I've been involved in these ransom-type things before ... rarely do they have a good outcome.'

'But we'll make sure this one does, sir.'

'We can't afford for anything to go wrong, though.'

'Don't get cold feet now – we'll get him, I know it.'

Bartlett returned home having been allowed by Greet to leave an hour earlier than usual. He turned his key in the lock and went into the hall. Topper poked his head through the banister at the top of the stairs and wagged his tail.

'Hello, boy – you been looking after Mother? All right – I'm coming up.'

Bartlett ascended the stairs and went into his bedroom, followed by Topper. Caroline was sitting in bed reading a book.

'Hello, George. I'm so pleased to see you – but you're early.'

'I missed you, princess – how are you feeling?'

'Much better, thank you, dear. I think that new medicine is helping.'

'I'm very glad to hear that. Where's Irene? In the garden?'

'No – she went along to take some beef tea to

Mrs Weekes. The poor old dear hasn't been well at all.'
'Mrs Weekes? Do I know her?'
'Yes. She lives out at Fenwick Road in that enormous house. You remember, she was at that summer fete last year. She makes jam, well, I don't suppose she can now with her arthritis so bad.'
'Yes, I remember. What time will she be back? She shouldn't have left you.'
'That's what she said but I insisted. She'll be back in about an hour. She can't stay shut in here all day long and it's such a beautiful evening – the air will do her good. She's been looking a little pale lately I fancy.'
'Is she all right?'
'Yes, George. I think she's a little lovesick.'
'Archie?'
'Yes – who else?'

Irene walked along and approached the turning into Fenwick Road. As she turned the corner, two men bumped into her, almost knocking her to the ground. She dropped her basket on the pavement, shattering the jar of beef tea. She bent to retrieve what remained.
'I'm so sorry.'
She looked up at the two men. One smiled at her and took her by the arm.
'Well you're a little sweetie, aren't you?'
He pushed her roughly to the other man.
'No – I think she's more your type than mine, Bill.'
The other man put his arms around her waist and kissed her on the cheek. Irene screamed.

'Don't – please let me go. No. Get off.'

She screamed again and began to cry. As Bill grinned at her she looked up at him and saw the smile turn to a grimace as his head was pulled back by his hair and he was spun around. Archie Boase lifted the man off his feet and dashed him against the wall. Turning quickly he swiftly landed a punch straight into the other's face. As he withdrew his fist, the man fell to the ground, bleeding from his nose.

'Turn around, please, Irene.'

Irene, terrified for herself and for Boase, obeyed. She heard more punches, what sounded like cracking bones, and much groaning. A minute later, Boase was by her side. He took her in his arms and as she looked over his shoulder she could see the two men, motionless on the ground.

'Archie ... are ... are they ... all right?'

'Who cares? You come with me.'

Boase led Irene across the road and into his lodging house. He entered the kitchen by the back door and sat her down at the table.

'I'm so glad I was there, Irene. I don't know what they might have done.'

Irene was still shaking.

'Here, have a little brandy – Mrs Curgenven has this to help her to sleep sometimes.'

Boase handed Irene a small glass and poured the brandy into it.

'Archie, I don't drink.'

'I know – but just have a drop. It'll help ... that was a terrible shock.'

She sipped the brandy and coughed. Boase smiled and took the glass from her. He stood her up next to him.

'Irene – well, I wanted to ask ... that is, I've been meaning to ask – well, I just had something a bit better than this planned but, well, seeing you just now, so helpless. I want to take care of you – always. Irene ... marry me?'

Irene looked into Boase's eyes and her heart melted.

'Archie, I thought you'd never ask.'

'Really?'

'I love you, Archie.'

'I really love you too, Irene. Is that yes then?'

'Yes. Yes. Yes.'

'I don't know what Irene would have done without you last night, Boase. She was so upset over what happened – thanks for bringing her home safely. It was lucky you were there.'

'Well, I'm glad I was, sir.'

Boase and Irene had made no mention to anyone of what else had passed between them. Boase wanted to speak to Bartlett himself and this wasn't really the right time while there was so much else going on. Inside he was bursting with happiness but couldn't say anything yet. No, he'd just have to keep this all to himself until the right moment, just get on with his job.

'Any sign of another note yet, Boase?'

'No, nothing, sir. It's still early. Do you think he'll do it?'

'I assume so – if he thinks there's a chance of getting the ring. I just hope the boy Stephen is all right.'

Boase fumbled in his pocket for an emergency

pork pie and laid it on the desk in front of him.

'That your breakfast?'

'Sort of, sir – I was a little late this morning. I only had time for toast, marmalade, a bacon sandwich, and some tea.'

'Only?' Bartlett couldn't remember himself ever having an appetite like that – not even when he was a young man.

'Yes, you definitely need a good woman to take care of you, my boy.'

Boase fidgeted in his seat. He knew exactly what he needed and didn't like deceiving Bartlett any longer than he had to. He said nothing but began, with a small penknife, to divide up his pork pie.

'Want a bit, sir?'

'No, thank you – you enjoy it. Wouldn't mind a cuppa though. Penhaligon back yet? I miss his tea – he's getting rather good at it.'

'No, sir. I think he's coming back tomorrow. His mother had two nights in hospital – he's very worried about her.'

'Well, so he should be – she's done a lot for him over the years, yes, they've had difficult times all right.'

A knock at the door was followed immediately by the desk sergeant's head poking around it.

'It's here, sir. The letter you've been waiting for, I think.'

'Who brought it?'

'Sorry, I didn't see anyone but it's been like Piccadilly out here this morning – anyone could have left it on the desk.'

'Well, how long ago did you notice it?'

'Just a couple of minutes, sir. The Flanagan

brothers were brought in again, found mixing it down on the Prince of Wales Pier ... drunk already. When I went back to the desk, there it was.'

Bartlett was opening the latest envelope and looking down on to the street below. A small boy was hurrying down towards the Moor. As he walked quickly, he turned and looked back at the police station.

'Boase – go after that boy down there, the one with the green trousers ... I've got a strange feeling he's the messenger.'

'Right, sir.'

Boase ran out of the door and on to the street. In the distance he saw the boy in the green trousers heading towards the library and Webber Street. He ran after him and got caught up in the market stalls which had been packed with people since about seven o'clock that morning. Negotiating his way through, he lost sight of the boy. He carried on to where Webber Street gave on to High Street. Looking up and down, he saw the boy, now running up the hill. Boase followed. Almost at the top he reached the Star and Garter. Enrico Trewavas was standing on the front step.

'Constable Boase – how lovely to see you. How are you?'

'Enrico – did you see a small boy in green trousers come past her a minute or two ago?'

'No – I saw him coming towards me ... but not past.'

'Where could he have gone?'

'Barracks Ope?'

Boase was gone already in the direction of the opening. He ran down the steps towards the sea.

The boy was nowhere to be seen. A fit man, Boase was now out of breath and his quarry was gone. He leaned against the wall for a moment. No – there was no one here, just two old rowing boats, a couple of crab pots, and some beer crates from Enrico's cellar. Boase, feeling the warmth of the sun and the strain of the exertion, suddenly felt a little peculiar. He loosened his collar and unbuttoned his jacket. The air would not come to him. He tried to take a breath but, no, he felt as though he were being strangled. This was all getting too much – a killer on the loose, the superintendent on and on all the time, the stress he had felt for poor Irene, and those awful men last night. Yes. Irene. Maybe Boase was just getting too excited. He'd need to calm down a bit. He sat down on one of the little upturned rowing boats and gazed out to Flushing. He felt a stone in his shoe and bent to remove it. As he leaned forward he saw something odd under the boat and right between his feet. He stood up from his seat and knelt to the ground. A piece of light blue linen was sticking out. Boase pulled on it. A button followed. And another. Crouching down further, Boase put his fingers underneath the wood and slowly lifted the boat. He dropped it back down quickly. A man's body was there. Boase composed himself and lifted it again. He could see an arm and a hand. He pulled gently on the sleeve. There was a finger missing. Donald Cook! But – why here?

Boase walked back up the steps and into the Star and Garter. Enrico came to the bar.

'Constable Boase? Archie – are you all right?

You look pale.'

'I'm fine, just had a bit of a turn, that's all. I'll be better in a minute. It's probably just the heat.'

'Let me get you a drink. Here, sit down.'

Enrico offered Boase a chair and went to fetch a jug of water. He poured the water and handed a glass to Boase who gratefully drank the contents.

'Enrico – would you please mind telephoning to the police station and asking Inspector Bartlett to come here?'

'You don't need to bother the inspector – I can walk you back to the station if you like.'

'Thanks but I really need him to come here.'

'Is there something wrong, Archie? Can I help you?'

'No, thanks – just the telephone call.'

'Very well.'

Enrico went into the back hall to the telephone. Boase finished the water and felt a little better. Enrico Trewavas was doing his best but this was something he couldn't help with.

Chapter Thirteen

George Bartlett arrived by car within about ten minutes of Enrico's telephone call. He ran into the Star and Garter to find Boase still sitting on the chair. He ran across to him.

'You all right, my boy? Enrico said you didn't look at all well.'

'I'm fine now, sir. Just got a bit overheated and

then I had a bit of a shock. Come with me.'

Bartlett followed Boase out of the pub and down into Barrack's Ope. They went across to the first boat.

'It's not good, sir. Look.'

Boase lifted up the side of the boat to reveal the body. Bartlett drew nearer and bent down.

'The head's gone, Boase. Did you see?'

'Well, no, but I did see the finger was missing – and we know where that ended up, don't we?'

'So, this is poor Donald Cook.'

'Looks like it, sir.'

Boase gently replaced the boat and stood up.

'You're still a bit shook up, aren't you, lad? Don't worry, I understand what awful memories this case must be stirring up. Let's get this mess cleaned up – I'll get someone down here now. Don't let anyone pass through this way until it's done.'

Boase waited by the boat until he was cleared to leave. He wandered back to the station, only pausing to look in a jeweller's window. He wondered what sort of engagement ring Irene would like. What did people do in this situation? Did they let their girl choose a ring – or was that the man's job? What if she didn't like what he chose? Mulling this all over in his mind, Boase reached the police station. Bartlett was in their office.

'There's a fresh cup of tea there for you, Boase. Drink it while it's hot – it'll revive you a bit.'

'Sir, you didn't get a chance to tell me what the note said – about the ring and about Stephen Penfold.'

'No, I didn't. He's blatant all right. I want to

speak to Sheila Parsons. This time she has to tell us what she knows or she won't see the light of day when all this comes out. Bring her up, Boase.'

Sheila Parsons sat in the chair next to Bartlett's window. She looked pale and thin. She had eaten barely anything since she had been kept at the station. Bartlett poured her a cup of tea.

'Sheila, look, I'm pleading with you now. This is all getting out of hand. We're close to catching the man who carried out these terrible acts – yes, we know now that there were two ... and I think you knew that all along too, Sheila. Your help now will only serve to help you in the future. And there's something else...'

Sheila looked up, enquiringly, at Bartlett.

'Jim Penfold is coming out of hospital tomorrow. He's in a bad way but he needs to be around for Angela.'

'How are they, Inspector Bartlett – really?'

'Jim is badly burned and it's affected his mind too – but I daresay he'll get over that in time. Angela's going to be all right too. But Jim is going to need your help in a way.'

'What can I do?'

'You can tell the truth. What you don't know is that your acquaintance – we have yet to discover his real name, is holding Stephen Penfold as a hostage.'

'What?'

Sheila couldn't understand how all this had happened – and now poor, dear Stephen was paying.

'It's true, I'm afraid. Listen to this.'

Bartlett pulled out the latest note and Sheila

and Boase sat very still as Bartlett read.

If you want to see this boy alive again then I want the ring. He's OK – for now. It's a simple exchange. Bartlett, I want you to bring the ring to Snow's Passage on Friday night. 11 o'clock. At the top of the lane is a derelict cottage. There is a hole in the side of the wall. Put the ring there. Turn round and you will see the boy. DO NOT BRING ANYONE WITH YOU.

'Inspector, if 'e's with that man, then 'e's in very grave danger. You must get 'im back.'

'You know all about this man, don't you, Sheila.'

Sheila took a sip of the tea and nodded.

'Yes, Inspector, I do. But I never in my worst nightmares could have imagined how terrible a man he is. 'E's a danger to everyone.'

'That's why you've been in here – he's not only dangerous, but clever and scheming. Now, start at the beginning ... and I want to know everything. All of it. Begin with his name and what he means to you.'

'Well, 'is name's Bert Bull. I was seein' 'im in London. We was together for about twelve months but I'd known 'im for years before that. I loved 'im and really thought we would be married. But 'e always 'ad some excuse – usually no money. I suppose you might say we was criminals together – nothing really bad, pickpocketing, shoplifting, and suchlike and I know 'e done some 'ouse breaking. Oh, yes – 'e could get in anywhere could Bert. I thought such a lot of 'im – but I knew quite soon that 'e 'ad problems, from the war like, you know – in 'is mind. Well, I didn't know 'ow bad 'e really was – not really until we come 'ere. I 'ad no idea.'

Sheila paused and sipped some more tea.

'I feel terrible, just awful, 'avin' lied to you – and now 'avin' caused so much trouble too.'

Bartlett pulled his chair closer to hers.

'But you've got the chance to do the right thing now, Sheila. Tell us everything that's happened.'

'Like I said. Bert never 'ad no money. 'E came back from the war – three times 'e was injured and each time they sent 'im back. There was no work for nobody let alone someone so bad. Every night, 'idin' under the bed, scared of 'is own shadow 'e was. Anyway, after 'e'd bin back a while 'e changed – for the worse. Getting violent over the slightest thing. We was still friends and eventually 'e asked me to be 'is girl. I said I didn't mind and I thought I could 'elp 'im. Well, 'e was hittin' me nearly every day, but I stuck with 'im. I spent a lot of time at sea so it worked out all right. Each time I came back I thought 'e might be a bit better and that we'd get married. I really loved 'im.'

Boase was almost beginning to sympathise with Bert Bull – why, he himself knew the horrors of war and felt lucky that he had returned able-bodied, well in his mind – and alive.

Sheila continued.

'As you know, I met Donald Cook when he was sailing back from Egypt. I wouldn't usually make such an acquaintance but 'e was really lovely to me. I told you before that I arranged for 'im to stay in London so that 'e could meet some friends before 'e came back 'ere. That's when 'e first showed me the ring.'

'So what happened when you came to Falmouth, Sheila? Did you come here with Bert?'

'I wanted to come on me own but Bert found me ticket and then 'e said 'e was coming with me. I told 'im I 'ad an interview but 'e insisted that 'e was comin' too.'

'Did you both have lodgings, Sheila?'

'Well, like I said before, I stayed behind the park until I moved in with Jim. That's 'ow I got involved with Mr Hargreaves – oh, I do hope 'e's better again now. I love cats, Inspector Bartlett.'

'Yes, I'm sure you do, Sheila. Do you know where Bert is staying now?'

'No, I don't. I don't know where 'e went when we arrived in Falmouth – 'e wouldn't tell me. An' then 'e just kept turnin' up – followin' me all over the place. No, I don't know where 'e's stayin' – if I did I'd tell you.'

Sheila began to cry and Boase offered his handkerchief.

'Come on Sheila, we might be getting somewhere now – you've got to tell us everything, at least for Stephen's sake.'

'Yes, I know. I'd do anything for those precious kids.'

'So what happened the night Desmond was killed?'

'I was in the Star and Garter – alone. Bert turned up asking me for money, 'e must 'ave followed me. We 'ad a drink together and then Donald and Desmond turned up. That was about eight o'clock. Donald started talking to me and Bert and he introduced us to Desmond – 'e seemed such a nice young man ... bit keen on the rich ladies though but 'e was very polite to me. Well, the pair of them started talking about Egypt. Donald really wanted Desmond to go back with 'im on 'is next trip but Desmond said 'e couldn't afford it. Donald had pots of money and even offered to pay the fare but I think Desmond said 'e already owed loads of money and was even goin' to ask 'is father for a loan to pay off some of 'is debts. Donald said if Desmond would go back with 'im then 'e would make sure 'e became very rich. That's when 'e brought out the ring. The landlady came over and 'e was showin' it to 'er too. Well, Bert saw it – Donald was telling everyone that it was priceless.'

'So how did this all end up with two young men being murdered? You're not telling us, Sheila.'

'I'm coming to that. I thought if I could steal that ring from Donald then I'd wouldn't 'ave to work again and Bert and me, well, we could afford to marry – I thought 'e'd get well again and we'd be like we were before. I admit, I've stole little things before but something like that, well – it could 'ave changed me life. So, I decided to try to get it. I told Bert that 'e'd 'ave to 'elp me – sort of distract Donald to give me a chance. We'd done stuff like that before together an' I thought that this would be just the same.'

'So, what did you do?' Bartlett could hardly believe that this girl had pulled the wool over his eyes for so long. She was in it up to her neck now though.

'Donald and Desmond 'ad both 'ad quite a few drinks and Donald decided to leave – 'e said 'e was going to look in on 'is uncle – sort of surprise 'im as 'e wasn't due back so soon. Well, Bert nudged me and just as Donald left, we got up and followed. We saw 'im outside. 'E stopped to light a cigarette and 'e started walking down the road. Bert ran up behind 'im and asked 'im outright for the ring. I said that 'e should 'and it over cos Bert could get very nasty – which wasn't a lie, I should know. Donald said no and Bert started to push 'im round a bit. I was getting' worried ... Bert was gettin' nastier and nastier. I pleaded with Donald to 'and it over – yes, I wanted the ring but I liked Donald an' I didn't want to see 'im get 'urt. Donald opened his bag where 'e'd put the ring but 'e said it was gone. Bert didn't believe 'im an' pushed 'im down that little alleyway – Barrack's Ope I think they call it. Well, I waited – I could 'ear a scuffle and that upset me a bit but I was afraid to say anything. They was gone for ages. A while later Bert came out – 'e said Donald 'ad collapsed but that was probably cos 'e'd drunk so much and that 'e'd searched 'is pockets and the ring definitely wasn't there. Apparently, Donald thought the only explanation was that Desmond had stolen it from 'im. 'E said 'e knew Desmond needed money but 'ad only to ask 'im and 'e would give 'im some. Bert asked 'im where Desmond lived and Donald told 'im; 'e must 'ave bin terrified. Oh!'

Sheila collapsed with her head in her hands and sobbed for all she was worth. Nothing Bartlett or Boase could say could console her.

'All right, Sheila, we'll have a little break for a minute or two – I can see how upsetting this all is. Here, let me open the window, it's very warm in here.'

Bartlett lifted the sash window and immediately a rush of warm and fresh air burst into the room. Boase fetched Sheila a glass of water and waited for the girl to continue. Bartlett looked at the clock – it was a quarter past five. If they were going to catch Bert Bull then they needed to have a plan in place. Stephen's safety was paramount.

'Oi! Want an apple?'

Bert Bull threw the fruit at the boy, Stephen Penfold. The boy looked at it then set it down on the table.

'Wot's wrong wiv it?'

'I want to go 'ome.'

'Well, you can't yet, see? That policeman 'as to get me something – an' give it to me tonight. If I don't get it, you're not goin' anywhere.'

'I want me Da and me sister. I want to go 'ome.'

'I want doesn't get.'

Bert Bull lifted a dirty blind up over the small-paned window. The day's light had almost gone.

'Why are you doin' this?'

'Cos I want to be rich.'

'Well, there's nothing I can do – I 'aven't got no money.'

'No – but you can 'elp me. Now, we just 'ave to sit tight an' then, if the policeman does as 'e's told, you can go 'ome. Well, if you've got an 'ome?'

'What do you mean?'

Bert Bull laughed.

'You'll see. Now, I'm off to collect me fortune. You be good and you'll soon be out of here.'

The wooden door slammed shut and Stephen was alone. He ran to the window and looked out. There was nothing familiar he recognised outside and no one around. He tried to lift the window but it was locked. He went to the door and turned the handle. The door opened. Stephen carefully pulled the door open further and looked out. There was a narrow corridor with another door at one end. A small oil lamp illuminated that area. Stephen was frightened but he didn't want to stay in here. It was cold and the smell was horrible – like rotten fish and with the fumes from the lamp making him feel ill. Looking both ways in the corridor, Stephen walked towards the end door. Turning to look over his shoulder, he tried the handle. The door was locked. He pulled again on the handle. Nothing. He rattled and pulled and the sound echoed up and down the corridor but the door wouldn't move. He looked up. Above and to one side of the wooden door was a small window and a ledge. Stephen, quite tall for nine years old, reached up to the ledge and pulled himself up. He got up further with the help of a large, rusty nail protruding from the wall and managed to slide along on to the ledge. As he looked through the small window he heard footsteps. He tried to slide further back into the ledge. Someone was coming this way. As the door, now beneath him, opened, the lamp was extinguished with the draught and the boy and the visitor were in darkness. Stephen didn't move, fearing even to breathe. He heard the wooden door close beneath him and felt the vibration as it slammed shut. He felt his hand lose its grip on the ledge and as he regained his position, the footsteps stopped. Someone had heard him. There was only darkness and silence. No one moved. Then the footsteps started again and disappeared into the distance. Stephen waited. Would the man find him gone and come for him? He listened. There were the footsteps again, returning. The man coughed and Stephen recognised the cough as that of his captor – he had heard it often since he had been here. Well, this was it. The man would find him now. He didn't move despite the cramp in his legs. Footsteps once more. Closer. Now they were underneath him. He could smell tobacco and alcohol. It reminded him of his father when he had been drinking. The wooden door opened once more, the man went through and it was slammed shut. Stephen breathed a full breath for the first time. He crawled along the ledge to the small window and pushed it. It opened. He couldn't see what was on the other side but only knew he wanted to get through. He squeezed his body through, ripping his trousers on a hinge. He carried on, fearing he would get stuck. After about three minutes he was on the other side. He dropped down and found himself on what seemed to be sand. He walked along the side of a hedge, not knowing where he was going. He was frightened and lost but he was out of that place and away from that man.

Bartlett loosened his collar – something which Boase had never seen him do before.

'Did you know that Donald was dead, Sheila?'

'No – Bert said 'e'd collapsed and I thought that was that. I 'ad no idea.'

'Then what did you do?'

'Well, Bert said we 'ad to find Desmond – 'ow it was all my idea and I couldn't give up now. I wanted to stop. I didn't want the ring no more if it meant 'urting people. Well, Donald 'ad told Bert that Desmond usually walked 'ome through Kimberley Park. Bert said we was to follow 'im. We caught up with 'im just as 'e reached the gates. They was locked so Desmond, and then we, went in through the 'ole in the fence. Bert walked up behind 'im and asked 'im for the ring. No, says Desmond, it's mine now. Anyway, Bert took out this huge knife – almost like a sword, it was. I never knew 'e 'ad that, Inspector Bartlett, 'onest I never. I think it was down 'is trouser leg. Desmond laughed at 'im and that made Bert worse. You'll never use that, says Desmond ... but 'e did. Oh, my God, 'e did. Cut 'is throat – it was so quick. I tried to run but Bert pulled me back. Check 'is pockets 'e says. I went through poor Desmond's pockets an' I found the ring. I told Bert it wasn't there. 'Old up yer open 'ands, he says. I did. What 'e didn't know was that I 'ad the ring on me little finger – I've done stuff like that 'undreds of times before. Oh, yes – I used to be a neat little pickpocket all right. Look again, 'e says. As I bent down to pretend to look ... that's when 'e did that ... to poor Desmond's 'ead. Well, I picked up Desmond's coat which was on the ground and just threw it down on top of 'im then I ran out of the park – I didn't even know where I was going. I knew Bert knew where I was stayin' be'ind the park – that's another reason I moved to Bar Terrace, to keep away from 'im.'

Boase sat all the while, amazed at this story unravelling before him. How could this young woman sit so calmly here and tell what had happened? Sheila continued.

'So, when your man saw me was when I went back to look for me glove. Bert's bin followin' me and saw me later the next day. I told 'im I was goin' back to London – 'e said 'e was comin' with me cos 'e knew I 'ad the ring and 'e'd stop at nothin' to get it. The followin' day I moved temporary into Jim's – then 'e asked me to stay. Bert saw me again – comin' in 'ere. 'E thought I'd grassed 'im up and said that I 'ad to give 'im the ring. 'E's bin following me ever since. Oh, what are you goin' to do about poor Stephen?'

Bartlett looked at the clock. It was twenty minutes to ten.

'Well, whatever we do, it'll have to be soon. You've got everything in place, Boase?'

'Yes, sir. All ready.'

'Right you are. Sheila, you're to stay here until this is all finished. You're not out of the woods by a long chalk but you'll stay here for now.'

'Please, Inspector Bartlett, can't I come with you?'

'Absolutely not. Right, I'll take the ring, Boase. I'll just put it in my pocket.'

The two men had one final cup of tea before their planned trip over to Snow's Passage. They left the police station at half past ten.

Stephen Penfold had reached Ponsharden and the Dissenters Burying Ground; not that he knew that. Stopping at the entrance to the cemetery he sat down on a step. He thought he recognised the area but was a little unsure. His father would never let him come this far on his own and he didn't ever remember being brought here. Something scurrying in the undergrowth startled him and he rose and went on his way in the direction of what he thought must be Falmouth. As he continued, rather worried to be alone in the dark and still more worried about what his father would say, he reached the top of Killigrew. Constable Johnny Bassett was checking the gates to the Recreation Ground. As he turned, his torch lit up the pale face of Stephen Penfold.

'Hey – you're a bit young to be out so late, aren't you?'

Stephen didn't answer.

'Where are you off to then? Are you lost? What's your name?'

The constable, used to resistance on questioning, bent down and put his hand on the boy's shoulder.

'Would you like a biscuit?'

Stephen nodded. He took the offering and ate it immediately.

'My name's Johnny – what's yours?'

'Stephen.'

'Stephen what? I'm Johnny Bassett.'

'Stephen Penfold.'

'Well I never! Stephen Penfold. Do you know how many people have been worried about you?'

Stephen shook his head and took another biscuit which was being offered.

'Well, I'd say, about a million.'

The boy giggled, knowing this to be impossible.

'Well, you have to come along with me, Stephen Penfold. Would you like a lift? Climb aboard then.'

Carrying the boy on his shoulders, Johnny made his way down Killigrew Street and headed for the police station.

Chapter Fourteen

As Johnny Bassett was approaching the police station with Stephen, who had fallen asleep on the constable's shoulders, Bartlett, Boase, Penhaligon and two other policemen walked across the Moor. It was twenty minutes to eleven. Bartlett had left instructions to send extra backup if he asked for it. The five of them should be enough, surely? As they entered Market Street, they took a sharp right turn up the steps onto Smithick Hill. This would bring them out just at the entrance to the old Snow's Passage. Bartlett was aware that he was supposed to be alone but he hadn't come just for Stephen, no, he wanted Bull too. With this in mind, he stopped his four companions, motioning to the two policemen and Penhaligon to cover both entrances to the hill. Penhaligon retraced his steps and the other two waited at the bottom where the hill met Market Street. Bartlett turned to Boase and whispered.

'I want you to wait here.'

'No, sir. I can't let you go up there on your own. It's too dangerous.'

'If you'd seen some of the things I've done, Boase, your hair would curl.'

'But, sir...'

'Wait here. I can't risk losing the boy.'

'If you need me, just whistle, sir. I'll be right here – I'll hear you.'

Boase, dissatisfied with this arrangement, stepped back into the shadows and watched as Bartlett made his way up Smithick Hill towards the small courts of which Snow's Passage was one. He turned as he reached the top and went down the steps to the meeting place.

Bartlett could see the derelict cottage in front of him. Feeling in his pocket, he checked that the ring was safe. He looked about him, there was no one there but him. A large cat ran across the court behind him, causing him to turn quickly. There were lights across the bay but this part of the town was quite dark. A little moonlight shone through but not enough to see anything by. Bartlett found the hole in the side of the old cottage, more through fumbling his way, and there he placed the ring. He turned, hoping to see the boy. As he waited the Parish Church bell indicated eleven o'clock. At the last strike, silence fell. Bartlett heard only one sound. Footsteps. He didn't dare to move. He knew the others were nearby and had every entrance covered. Bull mustn't get away but he had to have the boy with him. He stared into the darkness and waited as the footsteps got nearer to the location of the ring. He saw the shadow of a man revealed by the pale moonlight and moved a step nearer. He squinted through the darkness. As he watched, he plainly heard scrabbling in the side of the cottage wall. He knew the ring was taken and, so, he turned to find Stephen. There was no one there. He had been conned! Bartlett spun round and ran back up the court. The shadowy figure ran faster, up the steps and over the wall onto Vernon Place. As Bartlett stopped by the wall, he saw Bull running at top speed along the road. Turning to go back to Snow's Passage to look for the boy, he saw Boase running after the man. There wasn't much between them. Penhaligon, hearing Boase shout, had come along the road. He stopped by Bartlett.

'Penhaligon, quick. Boase needs help. They went up there. Run, man.'

Penhaligon followed on, along Vernon Place. He stopped opposite the public house on the corner. Boase and his quarry were nowhere to be seen. How had they just disappeared? Penhaligon, thinking he had missed the pair, retraced his steps. Before the pub, the road forked and ran along in front of the Vernon Place dwellings. Penhaligon guessed they must have gone that way and walked back down the hill.

Boase had also reached the pub on the corner, but on the other side from where Penhaligon had been standing. He stopped and leaned against the wall. He could hear music and laughter coming from inside the pub. It was over time but Boase had more important things to think about at the moment. Slowly he peered around the side of the pub from where he could see a railing and steps leading down, he guessed, to the pub cellar. He waited. He could clearly see a man's hat now, underneath the railings. Boase sprang forward, vaulted over the rail and landed on top of the man below. Both men collapsed to the floor. The other man was up again quickly and caught Boase with a blow to the cheek. Boase fell again. The man was facing him now and had picked up a large piece of wood. Both men waited. As the man ran forwards, wood aloft, Boase hurled a beer barrel towards him and the man, losing his footing, fell, face forwards onto the flagstones. Boase was on top of him and the man shouted out.

'All right. All right. I can't breathe. Let me up.'

'No chance, mate.'

At this the landlord of the pub came out of the cellar door and viewed the pair on the ground.

'Is that you, young Archie?'

Boase looked up and saw John May, a man he knew well, peering at him.

'Hello, John.' Boase was still panting. 'Sorry, I've made a bit of a mess of your yard.'

'Don't you worry, Archie. I'll fetch someone straight away. Looks like you've got your hands full.'

John May disappeared inside, leaving Boase and his prisoner, both still gasping, on the flagstones.

Hearing the police whistle, both policemen accompanying Bartlett and Boase earlier on that evening ran to the pub where they found Boase sitting on top of Bert Bull. A minute later, Penhaligon arrived and, finally, George Bartlett. The four stood peering over the railings down into the yard.

'Well done, Boase. Ask him what he's done with the boy – oh, and be sure to get that ring back off him ... it's not his.'

As Boase stood up, he dragged Bull by his

collar and to his feet. As the two men looked at each other, Bull grinned and put his hand behind his back.

'Archie – look out!'

Ernest Penhaligon had been the only one standing where he could see Bull's back. Bull drew a large knife from behind him. The blade flashed in the light being sent out from the cellar window. Boase stepped back. The yard was small and with the only means of exit either the stone steps or the cellar door. He reached for the handle. John May had taken the precaution of locking it from the inside. Boase looked towards the steps. Bull stood between him and them.

'Don't be a fool, man. You'll never get away with this.'

Bartlett began descending the stone steps.

'Stay back, sir. Stay back.'

'Hand it over, Bull.'

Bartlett was on the bottom step now, Bull between him and Boase. Bull held the knife in front of him. He stepped back and was now facing both men.

'Step away and let me go.'

'Where's the boy?'

'Gone. 'E scarpered.'

'Don't believe you. What have you done with him?'

'I told you. 'E escaped. I dunno where 'e is. Let me pass.'

Bull lunged at Bartlett who fell backwards over a beer barrel. The steps now unguarded, Bull ran up them. The three men at the top, seeing the blade flashing as it came towards them, parted and Bull was free. Boase ran up the steps behind him and followed him as he ran across the road.

'Stop, Bull. You can't get away with this.'

The others had followed and were now standing at the top of Jacob's Ladder.

'I've got the ring so just let me go. I don't know where the boy is – I told you, 'e ran away.'

Bull was backing away from the assembled group of policemen. Suddenly, he turned and ran down the first dozen or so steps of the ladder which had been behind him. He stooped and looked back up to where he could see Boase descending towards him. He held the knife in front of him.

'Stand away – I've used this before and I'm not afraid to use it again. Stand away.'

Bull turned and ran down still further. Bartlett came down behind Boase.

'Leave it, Boase, you'll get yourself killed. He's gone.'

Boase continued to descend. As Bull disappeared into the darkness and reached a small landing in the stairway no one above could see what happened next. Someone stepped out of the shadows and with one swoop, lunged forward towards Bull, sending him hurtling down the stone steps. The knife fell to the ground as the man plunged forwards. The men above heard a scream. And he was gone. Bartlett and Boase, followed by the others, came down to the landing. Bert Bull's assailant came forward.

'You!'

Both Bartlett and Boase stared hard at the person in front of them who had captured their man.

'Good evening, gentlemen. Yes, it is I, Leon Romanov, at your service.'

At this, Romanov bowed very low as he was accustomed to do. Now all of the men were staring at him. They looked towards the bottom of the stone staircase but could see nothing in the darkness. Boase hurried away from the others and descended still more steps. As he reached the next landing, there was Bert Bull. The man was crumpled in a heap, a huge gash on the side of his head was bleeding profusely. Boase bent down to check for any signs of life but didn't expect any. He was right. Bert Bull was dead.

Bartlett turned to Romanov, his eyes blazing.

'What the hell do you think you're doing, Romanov? You've just killed a man.'

'He killed himself, Inspector Bartlett. I was innocently standing here smoking when the madman rushed down the steps just as I emerged. I can hardly be held responsible if he tripped over my cane. My lovely cane – it belonged to my grandfather. It has a very interesting history.'

Bartlett couldn't believe how calm this man was – he had the feeling that this wasn't the first time he'd been involved in anything like this. Yes, this man was quite the expert.

'You'd better come to the station with us, Romanov.'

Bartlett grabbed the man's arm and the entire company descended Jacob's Ladder. At the bottom, he turned to the two young constables.

'Right, one of you stay here at the bottom, the other at the top – you don't let anyone pass ... do you hear? I'll get someone to come along to take him immediately. Boase – who's got the ring?'

'Well, Bull, I suppose, sir.'

'Never mind that now. We'll get it later. Come on.'

Leon Romanov sat in the chair next to Bartlett's desk.

'Inspector Bartlett, I hope you will not be taking this any further. This man merely met with a terrible accident – anyone can see that. He was not a nice person. Did he not murder horribly the two lovely young men that were Cooks?'

Boase looked up at this peculiar man sitting opposite him.

'Yes – but that didn't mean you had to kill him.'

'But he was getting away from you, was he not?'

Bartlett leaned across his desk, angry all over again.

'We would have got him.'

'Yes, I'm sure you would have. But, now – he has been got.'

Bartlett looked exasperated.

'You realise that you're not free to go, don't you?'

'But why not? I have done nothing wrong.'

'Despite what you think, you will have a lot of questions to answer later on today. You're going nowhere. Because of your actions, we might never locate a missing boy – Bull was probably the only person who could tell us the whereabouts of Stephen Penfold.'

Boase took Romanov out to Penhaligon who was in the lobby.

'Inspector Bartlett says he's to stay here tonight

– sort him out will you, Penhaligon?'

'Have you sent someone up to collect Bull?'

Bartlett had lit a pipe – something which he would never do at this hour. At three in the morning he should be in bed, asleep.

'Yes, they're going up there now, sir. I've sent Eddy and Rabone ... they're going to meet Dr Dancey on the Moor.'

'Right, well we need to sort out Sheila Parsons in the morning, too. She's safe from Bull – but not from the court. She's led us a merry dance and no mistake. She's by no means out of the woods.'

'Well, yes, but she didn't kill anyone, did she?'

'No, but by deceiving us, she put the Penfolds in serious danger.'

As the two finished the conversation about Sheila Parsons, there was a knock on the door. Boase walked over and opened it. Constable Johnny Basset stood there.

'I've brought someone to see you both.'

He stood aside and there was Stephen Penfold, tired and shabby after his ordeal.

'I've given him a cup of tea and some biscuits but he's extremely tired, sir.'

Bartlett walked over to the boy and placed his hand on his shoulder.

'Well, you must be Stephen Penfold – I can't tell you how pleased I am to see you, young man. Come in. I want to hear all about your adventure. We'll have a little chat and then I'll take you to see your father and sister – then you can get some sleep. I hear you're going to be staying with some relatives up at Penryn.'

Stephen yawned and shuffled from side to side.

'You must be exhausted. I'll soon have you back with your family. Sit down for a minute.'

Stephen sat on the chair next to the window and began to tell Bartlett what had happened to him and where he had been. It soon became apparent that Bull had actually been telling the truth when he said Stephen had escaped. Boase made notes and then prepared to take Stephen back to Jim Penfold who would be leaving hospital in the morning.

'I think after we've taken Stephen to the hospital we could go home for a couple of hours, Boase. I'd like to see Caroline and get forty winks if I can. I'm getting far too old for all this.'

Bartlett yawned and stood up. As he reached for his coat on the peg there was urgent knocking on the door. Bartlett opened it.

'What's all this you two – bit frantic, aren't you?'

Constables Eddy and Rabone stood in the doorway, agitated.

'Where's Bull now?'

'Well, sir. We don't know.'

'What do you mean ... you don't know?'

Boase came across to the door.

'Where is he?'

Eddy, the older man, spoke.

'We went up Jacob's Ladder with Dr Dancey, up to the landing as you directed. There was no one there.'

Bartlett put his coat back on the peg.

'No one there? What are you talking about, man?'

Rabone came forward.

'I'm sorry, sir. It's true. We, all three, looked up and down with torches. There's no one there. The two constables hadn't left their stations either. We asked them. They're still there now.'

Bartlett and Boase looked at each other aghast.

Bartlett pulled Stephen to him.

'I want one of you to take this boy up to his father at the hospital. Tell Mr Penfold that we'll speak to him tomorrow. The boy seems to be all right. Get an address of where he'll be. The other, stay here and let me know straight away if anyone comes in here with news. Greet will be here at nine – he's going to be livid. Boase, come with me.'

As Bartlett and Boase crossed the Moor towards Jacob's Ladder, Bartlett spoke first.

'Boase – what's going on? You said he was dead.'

'Sir, I couldn't detect any signs of life. I know it was dark but I felt him all over – there was no pulse.'

'Well, he's either been moved – or he's not dead at all and you've been mistaken.'

'Sir, I'm so sorry.'

As they reached the bottom of Jacob's Ladder, the young constable stepped forward.

'Did you see anything?'

'No sir. No one's come past me. I haven't moved since you were here.'

Bartlett and Boase went up and down the staircase. No one was there.

'If he was just stunned, Boase, he might have got over the wall on that landing. But I can't believe it.'

'Sir, I feel terrible. I'm so sorry.'

Boase felt humiliated to have made such a stupid mistake.

'Well, sorry's no good now. We've got to find him. If he had such a bad head injury he can't have gone far. He must be nearby.'

'He must be strong as an ox, sir.'

'I think we already know what he's capable of.'

At twenty minutes past four, Bartlett turned his key in the lock at Penmere Hill. Topper heard the latch and came across the hall to meet his master.

'Topper, old boy. I'm so glad to see you. You always wait for me, don't you? You get back into bed – it's very late, well, very early. I'm off upstairs. How's your mother? Have you been looking after her?'

Topper sat in his bed, listening, with his head cocked on one side. On his master's instruction, he lay down and closed his eyes, satisfied that his family were now all at home. Bartlett tiptoed upstairs and across the landing to his bedroom. The door was ajar. He went round to the side of the bed. Caroline turned.

'George.'

'I'm sorry to wake you, princess. I was trying to be quiet.'

'I wasn't asleep.'

'Are you ill again?'

'No. I'm quite well. I thought you'd be back before now. What time is it?'

'About half past four.'

'George, that's very late. Come and lie down.'

Bartlett took off his jacket and shoes and lay on top of the eiderdown next to his wife. He leaned across and kissed her forehead.

'I'll have to get up again soon. I've got a lot to do. Oh my word. What a night!'

Chapter Fifteen

A weary duo sat in the office at Berkeley Vale the next morning at half past eight. Bartlett and Boase, bleary-eyed from the strain of earlier events, sat drinking tea to try to revive themselves for the day ahead. Bartlett lit his pipe and, perching on the corner of his desk, looked out of the window on to the street below. Boase sat behind his own desk and unwrapped a small parcel. He laid it open on the desk.

'Hungry, sir?'

'What have you got? I didn't have time for breakfast. That's not like me at all. Every man should eat breakfast.'

Archie Boase looked amazed. In all the time he had known George Bartlett, Boase had always offered a share of his food and, at every turn, had politely been declined. Bartlett wandered across to him.

'Well, I've got two hard-boiled eggs, a mutton sandwich, and some chocolate.'

Bartlett dithered.

'It's a bit early, but ... well, go on, I'll have a bit of your sandwich.'

'Take it all, sir.'

'No. Half will do – thank you, Boase.'

Bartlett took the sandwich and sat behind his desk to eat it. He suddenly held the sandwich aloft.

'We can't sit here eating while this man's still at large. Get Sheila Parsons. She might know the sort of places he'd go to.'

Boase left the room to fetch the girl from downstairs. Five minutes later, he returned.

'Sir, sir. She's gone.'

Bartlett turned to look at his assistant.

'Gone?'

'Yes, sir. I just checked with Coad. He said that Greet was in at about seven this morning and heard what had happened earlier. Apparently he told everyone that he was glad to see the end of this case and now that Sheila Parsons wasn't in danger, she could go.'

'He had absolutely no right to do that. She's still implicated in all of this and she has to take her punishment. And besides that, she could now be in terrible danger if we don't find that man.'

Bartlett rose from his chair.

'I'm going up – Greet needs to be told. He's forever meddling in my cases and I've had enough.'

'Sir, Coad says he was only here for twenty minutes – he's had to go to court in Truro. He won't be back until tomorrow.'

Bartlett sat back down and fiddled with a pencil.

'Did Coad say where she's gone?'

'No. I suppose she'll try to find Jim Penfold? We could ask him. He'll be leaving the hospital later this morning.'

'That's an idea. We'll do that, Boase.'

At eleven o'clock, Bartlett and Boase made their way up to the hospital at Killigrew. They were very aware that a huge manhunt was now underway to find Bull. Messages had been sent around the county with a description and orders to approach him cautiously. The pair had other things on their mind now – making sure that Sheila was safe. The nurse at the hospital showed them in to Jim Penfold's ward. He was just waiting to see the doctor and was spending the time talking to Angela and Stephen. Bartlett was pleased to see the little family reunited again.

'Good morning, Jim. How nice to see you up and about.'

'Hello, Inspector Bartlett, Constable Boase. I'll be glad to be out of here, I can tell you. They're all lovely but I'm ready to get out and about again now. I've got somewhere nice to stay – my cousin, Edna is taking us all in until the house is repaired. She's got a place up in Penryn. It's far too big for her and she'd be glad of the company. Anyway, what brings you here?'

'Well, I'm very pleased to hear that things are working out for you, Jim. We have got a problem though. We need to find Sheila. Have you seen her this morning?'

'No. I thought she was at the station with you? Is everything all right?'

'I can't give you details but, no, she's not with us and we really need to find her. She was released this morning – apparently, and I just thought she'd come straight here.'

'Is she in danger, Inspector?'

'Well, if I'm honest, she could be.'

'Anything I can do?'

'Just get better – and let us know immediately if you hear from her.'

'You've got me worried too now.'

'Let us do the worrying – and get well. See you again, Jim. Bye kids.'

Bartlett and Boase walked back down Killigrew Street. In their office, Bartlett looked at Boase.

'Where is she? Greet just let her walk out of here and she could be anywhere. She's still a criminal – what on earth does he think he's playing at?'

'I don't know, sir, but I feel awful at making such a stupid mistake.'

'Well, maybe – but it was dark and you were under pressure. Don't worry – just think how we can get round all this.'

Boase was grateful for Bartlett's understanding – he didn't think he would be so tolerant in the same position.

'What it does mean is that we'll have to let Romanov out. He hasn't killed anyone, so it seems.'

'Yes. But shall I tell him to stay in Falmouth, sir?'

'Yes – you should. At least until this is cleared up. I must confess, that was a nifty bit of work on his part – but don't tell him I said so.'

Bartlett walked back home later than usual, despite his previous late night. He thought as he made his way along. Romanov was out. Sheila had disappeared. Bull was nowhere to be found and could be plotting ... well, who knows what, at this very minute? Irene saw him come through the gate and ran to open the front door. She hugged him.

'Hello, Dad. You look exhausted. I've just made a pot of tea.'

'Well, thanks, Irene, but if you don't mind, I fancy a glass of my beer.'

'All right, Dad. I'll get it for you. Mum's in the parlour. She's feeling so much better. Topper's keeping her company.'

Irene took Bartlett's coat from him. He went into the parlour. Caroline was sitting in her armchair with Topper at her feet. The dog, on seeing his beloved master, rose and walked over to greet him with a lick on the hand.

'All right, Topper – you been looking after your mother? You're such a good boy. Hello, princess. Irene says you're feeling better?'

'Hello, dear. Yes, I am. I really think those new pills are working for me.'

Bartlett pulled a small chair across and sat next to his wife. He took her hand in his.

'No one is more pleased than me to hear that, princess. Irene is just getting me a drink.'

Bartlett yawned long and hard.

'George, you're exhausted. Why don't you go and have a lie down. You've barely had any sleep.'

'I'm not going to bed at eight o'clock. Anyway, I'm feeling rather hungry – I must be turning into Boase.'

'I'll ask Irene to get you some supper. We've already eaten – we didn't know what time you'd be back – I hope you don't mind?'

'Of course not. Any leftovers?'

At that moment, Irene came in with a bottle of Leonard's and a glass.

‘Now, that’s what I really need. Thank you, Irene. Anything to eat?’

‘Course, Dad. Hot or cold?’

‘I don’t mind – anything.’

‘There are some cold potatoes – the ones you grew – ham, cheese, pickle. Or I can cook you something hot, if you prefer?’

‘No – cold is fine. Any of those lovely bread rolls you made?’

‘Yes. Shall I bring it all in here on a tray so you can sit with Mum?’

‘Yes please – that’d be lovely.’

Bartlett could never think of anything nicer than sitting with his lovely wife.

In Melvill Road, Boase had just returned home. Mrs Curgenven had gone to visit a friend but had kindly left a cold supper. Boase demolished it in less than ten minutes and went back to the pantry to hunt out anything else that he might have missed. His landlady was so good to him – he had the run of the place and was very well fed. What more could he ask for? As he rummaged in the cupboards he wondered what could have happened to make this case go on for so long – he blamed himself and he knew Bartlett did too ... he was just being charitable. He thought about what he could do to make this right while he extracted two sticky boiled sweets from deep in his jacket pocket. Well, maybe the first thing would be to get some sleep. He couldn’t think straight while he was so tired. And so it was that, at ten past nine, Archie Boase went up to his room and fell asleep, fully clothed, on his bed.

Three days had passed since Bull had disappeared. The desk sergeant stopped Bartlett on his way to his office.

'Sir, I have a message here from Jim Penfold. He says would it be possible for you or Constable Boase to pay him a visit – maybe later on today, He would come down himself only the doctor has told him he's to stay in for at least another week.'

'Well, I'm quite busy, I'll ask Boase to go along and see him later. What's his address?'

'I've written it down, sir. Here you are.'

Boase was already at his desk drinking some tea. He looked up as Bartlett entered.

'Morning, sir. Cuppa?'

'I wouldn't say no – thank you, Boase. Any news?'

'No, sir. Nothing.'

'Would you go along to Penryn this afternoon – Jim Penfold wants to see you. I can't go, I've been summoned to see Greet. He's really going to haul me over the coals, I know it. Here's the address – it's up on the Helston Road.'

'Right you are, sir. I'll go up at about six this evening – will that be OK?'

'I'm sure it will – but that's in your own time?'

'Yes, sir. I know but I've got such a lot to do today.'

'Fair enough. What are we doing this morning?'

'Well, we've got to talk to Romanov and try to sort that mess out. Find Sheila Parsons I suppose – easier said than done.'

'Right, get someone to ask Romanov to come in – he's still at the Falmouth Hotel. I'll be seeing

Greet at three o'clock so that gives us a bit of time to see if we can find out anything about the girl.'

At a few minutes after six o'clock, Boase was knocking at the door of a rather smart house on the Helston Road in Penryn. It was opened by Stephen Penfold.

'Hello, Stephen. How are you now? Got over your adventure? I'm here to see your Dad.'

The boy showed Boase into the large parlour which looked out over a lawn with a pond in the centre. Jim Penfold was sitting in the window. He stood up when Boase entered the room.

'Don't get up, Jim. Please sit down.'

'You too then, Constable Boase. Stephen, go outside with Angela – see if you can find any fish.'

The boy ran outside to find his sister and immediately a large slap was heard followed by crying.

'I don't think they two will ever get on, you know.'

Jim banged hard on the window pane and the howling stopped.

'What did you want to see me about, Jim?'

'It's Sheila. I bin worried ever since you said she wasn't with you no more. I 'aven't seen her.'

'I thought you would be the first person she would come to.'

'So did I. She knows where I am – Edna left a message at your station. I 'ope she got it.'

'She did – I gave it to her myself.'

'So, where can she be?'

'Can I talk to Stephen?'

'Yes. Of course. Stephen. Stephen – come back in. Constable Boase wants to talk to you.'

The boy came running in from the garden.

'Stephen, you remember when Inspector Bartlett was asking you about where you had been? Well, we couldn't find anywhere like that and I would really like to find the place where you had that little adventure. There's that horrible man and I really want to find him. Do you think you would be able to help me?'

Stephen nodded.

'Will that be all right, Jim?'

'Of course – I know Stephen will be safe with you. What are you thinking about?'

'I'm not exactly sure – but if I could take Stephen with me, it would be a help. I'll bring him back before it gets too late.'

'That's no problem. If you think it might help Sheila then you go ahead.'

'Thanks, Jim. Do you have a telephone here?'

'Yes.'

'I'd like to call the station just to tell Inspector Bartlett where I'm going.'

Boase established that Bartlett was still with Greet and left a message asking him to meet up before he went home.

Boase strolled back through Penryn with Stephen and headed for the river. The boy chatted all the while.

'I like Sheila. Me dad likes 'er, too.'

'I know he does. I'd like to know where she is. I've asked lots of people and no one has seen her.'

''As she gone to London? I've never been to London. She told me it was really big.'

'Well, I've been to London once – it's very, very big. If she's gone there we'll never find her.'

The pair reached the river and Boase sat on the wall and waited. He hoped Bartlett would have the message by now and soon be on his way. Hopefully he'd be glad of an excuse to terminate the meeting with the Superintendent. He didn't have long to wait. A car driven by Penhaligon drew up alongside Boase and Stephen and both Bartlett and driver alighted.

'What's all this about, Boase? Hello, Stephen. You all right?'

'I've been to see Jim and he's really worried about Sheila. He thought she would have contacted him by now but he hasn't heard from her. I've been asking around for days and absolutely no one has seen her. She's so distinctive with that red hair and peculiar clothing.'

'So why are we here?'

'Well, I'm wondering if Bull's got her.'

'Yes ... but why are we here?'

'Because if you remember, Stephen said that Bull had kept him around here somewhere. That's why I've brought him.'

Stephen was standing in the mud throwing stones into the river.

'But it might not be safe if Bull's here.'

'I know, but Jim was happy to let me bring him – if it meant possibly finding Sheila. I said I'd return him safely before too long.'

'I suppose it's worth a try. It's your idea but we do this my way.'

'All right, sir.'

'Get Penhaligon to go back to the station and

fetch a couple of men back here for assistance – just in case we find Bull. Tell him he can take Stephen for a ride in the car.'

Boase did as he was instructed and then stood with Bartlett awaiting Penhaligon's return.

Bartlett lit his pipe and wandered up and down alongside the river looking at the boats which were moored there. Boase sat on the wall enjoying the evening sunshine and hoping for an end to all of this soon. What would Irene think if she knew how he'd messed up? How useless he was? He took a small bar of chocolate from his pocket and offered half to Bartlett.

'No thanks, Boase. I'll ruin my supper – if I ever get home, that is. What can be keeping Penhaligon?'

'Maybe he's having trouble getting someone to come over, sir.'

'What are you hoping to achieve here, Boase?'

'I'm not sure, sir. But you know when you just feel something? I'm hoping that Stephen will show us where he was held. If Sheila's not there we might have a chance of catching Bull. We haven't seen him around – no one has. If he hasn't left the county, what better place than where he held Stephen?'

'Let's hope you're right. I really want to wipe that sneer off Greet's face. He gave me a right pasting today, Boase. He wasn't holding back. I was just about at the end of my patience when you telephoned.'

'I guessed that would be the case, sir.'

'I can tell you, it's a good job I'll be finishing soon. Not before time.'

'You're not going anywhere yet, sir. Are you?'

'I'm seriously considering it, my boy. All the trouble we go through – it's all right for you, you're just a youngster. Me? Well, I've been doing this for years and, if I'm honest, I'm worn out. This latest bout of Caroline being ill again – she really had me worried, and no error. No, I think the time is coming when we want to spend a bit more time together. She's had years of worrying about me – especially working up in London. No, it's not good for either of us.'

'But – but what about me?'

'Well, you'll do all right. They'll find someone to put you with. You'll have your own assistant before you know it – and a promotion and pay rise.'

'I suppose so. But don't go just yet.'

Bartlett grinned

'We'll see. Well! Look over there. That's Pasty Nine Lives. I don't believe it.'

'Who?'

Boase looked across and saw an old man in a red jersey and a peaked cap sitting in a small rowing boat on the shore.

Bartlett wandered over to him and Boase followed behind, curious.

'Pasty – how good to see you. I haven't seen you for years. How are you?'

'That you, Mr Bartlett, sir?'

'Yes, it's me, Pasty.'

'I thought I recognised the upcountry accent – sort of foreign.'

Bartlett shook the hand which was extended in his direction.

'How are you keeping, Pasty?'

'Well, I can't complain, Mr Bartlett – no one listens.'

Bartlett chuckled.

'You're looking well.'

'I'm not bad – me eyesight is very poor though. I can't see much these days – just as well I know me way around.'

'There's no one knows this stretch of the river like you, Pasty. How long have you worked here?'

'Gettin' on for seventy years, Mr Bartlett. Me father used to bring me 'ere when I was no more than three year old. I started workin' with 'im from the age of thirteen. I always knew I wanted to work on the river. I love it round 'ere. All these little creeks and nooks. I wouldn't want to be anywhere else in the world. I 'ope I die 'ere.'

'Well, not just yet, eh?'

'Well, I'm nearly eighty-two. It's bin a nice life, really. Bit 'ard sometimes but I wouldn't 'ave 'ad it any other way. Mind, I don't see much but I understand things.'

'Pardon?'

Bartlett sat down next to the old man. 'What do you mean, Pasty – you understand things?'

'Ha! People think that I'm just an old fool, an' I let 'em think it. But I know. There's always something 'appening on the river, Mr Bartlett. Thievin', courtin', fightin' – I've even seen a man killed 'ere when I was younger. Yes, it all 'appens on my little river. Only a couple of days ago I thought a young woman was goin' to be killed – right 'ere. Right where we're sittin' now, Mr Bartlett.'

'Whatever do you mean?'

'I see things. Not clearly, but at my age you get

to know enough to know what's what.'

'What did you see, Pasty?'

'A courtin' couple. They was standin' 'ere – I'd just gone over there, in the 'edge for a minute, you know. When I was on me way back they was really arguin'. She was teasy as an adder – I think 'e was tryin' to 'ave 'is way with 'er, there's plenty of that goes on round 'ere, and she wasn't interested, or changed 'er mind. Well, she was cryin' and 'e was sort of draggin' 'er. I called out – I thought 'e must be 'urting' 'er somethin' terrible. Me legs is bad an' by the time I got 'ere, they was gone.'

'What did they look like?'

'I couldn't say – I could only 'ear them. Come to think of it, 'er voice sounded a bit like yours, Mr Bartlett. Me eyes are aren't good enough for seein' much, like I told you.'

'Didn't you think to tell anyone?'

'No. I never – I told you, things 'appen like that 'ere all the time. A young man gets a girl down 'ere in the dark – sometimes she says yes, sometimes, no. That's the way of the world, Mr Bartlett. Yes, women are just like boats – all right to look at but you never really know until you've started 'er up and then you find out she needs too much work.'

Boase, glad of a diversion, turned as he heard a motor car coming along the road from Falmouth.

It was just after eight o'clock when the car drew up and Penhaligon, two more constables, and Stephen stepped out.

Bartlett said goodbye to Pasty and walking back up to the road, acknowledged the men.

'You took your time, Penhaligon.'

'I'm sorry, sir. Superintendent Greet wanted to

know why you needed us all – I tried to explain.'

'He's still there? I thought he'd have gone home by now.'

'No, sir. He's still there in his office.'

'Right. Now listen to me. You do as I say. No changing anything. Penhaligon, you take care of Stephen the whole time. You don't let him out of your sight – do you hear me?'

'Yes, sir.'

He turned to the two constables.

'You two. Do exactly as I say. I don't really know what's going to happen – possibly nothing but you follow my orders. If anything happens to Penhaligon, you take care of the boy. Got it?'

They both nodded while Penhaligon looked at Bartlett and then at Boase, perplexed and not a little worried at what event might befall him.

Chapter Sixteen

Bartlett, having given each man instructions – as well as he could, seeing that he himself didn't really know entirely what was going on, led the way followed by Penhaligon holding on to Stephen's arm. The others were behind with Boase at the rear. As they made their way through the mud, Bartlett stopped and waited for Boase. Separating him from the group he spoke quietly.

'Did you hear what Pasty said?'

'About the couple?'

'Yes – do you really think it was them?'

'Dunno, sir. Like the old man said, there's loads of couples coming down here all the time – but he said she spoke like you. Shame he couldn't see them.'

'Yes. If it is them then you might be right and Bull's taken Sheila to the same place that he had Stephen locked up in.'

'This is all my fault, sir.'

'No time for that now, Boase. We need to find out where Stephen was held.'

Bartlett went across to the boy.

'Do you recognise this place, Stephen?'

Stephen shook his head.

'No, there aren't so many buildings here.'

'What sort of buildings?'

'Big, smelly ones – made of wood.'

'Like big sheds?'

'Yes, but really smelly.'

'What was the smell, Stephen. Fish?'

'No – it was like Dad's old motorcycle.'

Bartlett turned back to Boase.

'Oil?'

'Could be, sir. Some repair their boats here – could be oil.'

The group walked on hoping that Stephen would soon recognise something from his previous experience.

'Boase, why do you think this place is round here?'

'Because I went back over my notes and made a small map with the things that Stephen was able to recognise on his way back to Falmouth that night. Everything he said pointed to him having started out about here. It's got to be right, sir. The only thing I'm worried about is that we find the place and there's no one there.'

'OK – we'll keep on. What time did you tell Jim you'd return the boy? Much further and we'll be in Truro.'

'I just said not too late.'

Bartlett looked at his watch. It was already nine o'clock and the light was fading. They walked further until Stephen tugged Penhaligon's sleeve. He was pointing across the river to the other shore. Across the narrow stretch of river was a small group of buildings. Boase turned to the boy.

'Is that it, Stephen? Is that where you were locked in?'

Stephen nodded. There was no apparent way of reaching the sheds apart from by boat. Bartlett looked at Boase.

'Well, I'm not swimming over there.'

'So how did Stephen get from there to here – he didn't swim?'

Stephen ran on ahead to a clump of bushes and began to scrabble through. Bartlett grabbed him by the seat of his shorts.

'Just a minute, young man. Is that how you got out? Through here? We can't crawl through there, Boase – we're grown men. Stephen could only just scrape through.'

Boase bent down and pulled aside the undergrowth. He stamped on the ground a few times.

'It's wood, sir. I've seen people crossing here at low tide – I think it's a series of planks in the mud. That must be how Stephen crossed. The tide is higher now and they're submerged. We'll have to steal a boat, sir.'

'Steal a boat? Are you mad?'

'Possibly, sir, but Bull could be over there with Sheila and we need to get there.'

Bartlett looked around him. There were several small rowing boats nearby. He pointed to one.

'OK – that one. But we bring it straight back. Dear me, I hope Greet doesn't get wind of this.'

As the boat was launched into the water, the moon came from behind the clouds and lit their way. All six got in and the constables took the oars. The water swished as the little boat made its way the short distance across the river. Boase hoped he'd made the right decision. No one else had suggested anything so it was worth a go. Within a few minutes the constables were pulling the boat up onto the shore and the small group had assembled under cover of some trees. Bartlett turned to Boase.

'We're quite close now – how do we know which one?'

Stephen was looking at the furthest shed. He pointed to it.

'It's that one. I remember, it's that one.'

The group quietly made its way along the shore towards the building. It was almost dark now.

'How shall we do this, sir?'

'I think we should leave the boy here. Tell him to hide behind that boat – over there and not to move until we come back for him. We'll go in the front – if we can get in. Send the others around the back.'

Boase gave Stephen a hard-boiled egg and, leaving the boy safely behind the boat, the five men walked towards the front of the building.

'Right, Boase, you stay with me – you three, spread out around the back. Don't let anyone get past you, no matter what. Be careful – if Bull's here, he'll probably be armed.'

The three constables carefully made their way past the front of the shed and to the back. Bartlett and Boase stood at the corner of the building and waited. The front had two large wooden doors about fifteen or twenty feet in height. The pair approached. The doors were padlocked shut. To one side was a narrow gap which had an iron gate across it. Boase pointed to it silently. Bartlett could just about make out the gesture and both men moved to the side. Boase pushed the gate open. It creaked. Bartlett nudged him and both men waited silently. There was no noise and Boase tried again to open the gate wide enough for them to get through. They were in! A wooden door was ahead of them. Boase tried the handle. The door was locked. Exasperated, Bartlett rummaged quietly in his coat pocket and withdrew a penknife. He handed it to Boase. Working quickly and silently, Boase manipulated the knife back and forth along the edge of the wooden door and prised it open. He whispered low.

'That was surprisingly easy.'

He pushed the door open and both men entered into what appeared to be a large workshop. The oily smell was apparent now. There were a couple of small boats on the far side and numerous tools and cans of oil were thrown casually about the floor. The men peered through the gloom. No one was about. Boase stepped forward into the darkness and walked into what felt to him like an oil drum. The offending object fell against the wall and Boase grabbed it to prevent any further noise. As he did so, he felt cloth under his hand. He turned to Bartlett and whispered.

'Petrol ... looks like someone's been burning rags – or clothes?'

They carefully walked over to the other side where the boats were. In the wall was another small door. Boase pushed this open with ease and the pair went through to the other side. They found themselves in a long corridor. As they made their way along, suddenly there was a loud crash and a light appeared a few feet in front of them. Feeling an aperture in the wall, Boase grabbed Bartlett and dragged him into it. They heard a door open at the other end of the corridor and footsteps came closer. Bartlett and Boase drew themselves tighter to the wall as the footsteps came nearer still. Just as Boase was about to lunge forward and reveal his whereabouts, another door opened and the footsteps disappeared. Both men sighed. Bartlett whispered to Boase.

'Do you think that was Bull?'

'Dunno. We should move.'

The two advanced further down the corridor to where the light had been seen a few minutes earlier. It was now dark again. Boase pointed to another door. They went slowly towards it. Boase tried the handle and the door pushed open. This time they were in a much smaller room. The moon was filtering through the grimy skylights and showed up another boat and a small motorcycle. Suddenly a muffled sound came from the corner of the room. The two men looked at each other and listened. Again, the same sound. Boase walked across the room to the boat. He peered in. There was a tarpaulin. All at once the moon disappeared and they were in darkness once more. Bartlett came to his aid and offered a box of matches. Boase took one from the box and struck it. Leaning over the boat, he pulled the heavy tarpaulin. As he lifted the match he clearly saw a face looking up at him. The match burnt his finger and he dropped it. He lit another. Again, the face looked up at him. Bartlett pulled the tarpaulin out of the boat and as the moon returned to beam through the skylight, Sheila Parsons could be clearly seen. She didn't move.

'Is she all right, sir?'

'I think so. Wait a minute. Help me to lift her out. Take this tape off her mouth, too.'

As the two men tried to pull the girl from the boat, they heard a door open. They both turned. There in the doorway, the lantern he was holding illuminating his grinning face with the gold tooth, stood Bert Bull.

'Well, if it ain't the meddlin' police again.'

'We've got you this time, Bull – finally.'

'Not yet you 'aven't. I was just comin' in to 'ave a word with Sheila. Now you've interrupted me. I really don't like bein' interrupted.'

At this, he drew the large knife from behind his back, at the same time dropping the lantern to the floor. The room was dark again. Sheila screamed. Bartlett and Boase could see nothing. Boase heard Bull moving sideways across the back wall. One step at first. Then another. He pushed Bartlett back to the boat where Sheila was standing.

'Stay there, sir.'

Boase struck a match. The blade of Bull's knife flashed in the light. Boase, realising that Bull was quite close to him, dropped the match. Moving in a circle round the room, Boase lit another. Bull had retreated to the door again.

'Going somewhere, Bull?'

At that, Bull leapt forward in Boase's direction. Boase heard the rush of air as the blade cut through it. In an instant he had lit another match and tossed it forward. It fell into the trickle of lamp oil where Bull had dropped the apparatus on the floor. Combined with the amount of flammable substances present in the room, the lamp exploded into a ball of fire. The flames enveloped Bull. He ran back and forth, screaming. As the fire took hold of him, he fell to the floor and soon the room was dark again. Boase grabbed Sheila by the hand and pulling Bartlett by his sleeve, ran from the room, back through the corridor, across the large boat workshop and out into the side alley. As they ran through the iron gate and round to the front of the building, Boase released Sheila's hand and fell to his knees, choking from the toxic fumes that he had inhaled. Bartlett was coughing too. The three constables, hearing the noise, ran to the front of the shed and to the assistance of Bartlett, Boase and Sheila. Penhaligon sat Sheila up against a tree and, as she looked up, there was Stephen Penfold. She lifted her arms up and the boy ran to her. Boase stood up.

'You all right, my boy?'

'I think so – thanks, sir.'

'That was some do, wasn't it?'

'I thought he had me with that knife, sir.'
'Well, you did the only thing you could.'
'I hope so, sir.'
'It was you or him, Boase. Just you remember that.'
'Thank you, sir.'
'Now, we need to see about getting this young man home, Penhaligon. I suppose the boat is the only way again?'
'Yes, sir.'
Penhaligon led Sheila and Stephen to the water's edge and the assembled group boarded the boat. As the two constables rowed, Boase slumped forward, exhausted. Bartlett nudged him.
'Wake up, Boase. We're here now. Come on.'
As the boat was pulled up onto the shore, someone stepped forward and offered his arm to Boase. Bartlett squinted at the volunteer.
'Romanov? You again?'
'Yes, Inspector Bartlett. It is I, Romanov. At your service.'
The customary bow followed and Romanov led Boase back up to the road and to the car.
'Well, I'm not even going to ask how you knew about this, Romanov. All the same I'm pleased to see you.'
At this, Romanov removed a flask from the small case he was carrying, together with two cups. He poured from the flask into the cups and handed one to Boase, the other to Sheila.
'Thanks, Romanov. I don't really drink.'
'Drink it, Boase – you've had a shock. Just drink it.'
Boase drank the colourless liquid and winced.

Sheila's cup was already empty and she was wiping her mouth with the back of her hand. Romanov had a taxi waiting and offered its use to return Stephen back home to his father.

At half past five, the exhausted group returned to the police station and headed for Bartlett's office. Bartlett lit his pipe.

'Well, that's that, I suppose.'

Romanov came forward.

'Inspector Bartlett, do you think it will be all right if I pay a visit to Dr Cook?'

'Well, I don't see why not, Romanov. You're a friend of the family. Yes, he'd probably be pleased to see you.'

'I should like very much to see him. I should have visited sooner only I have been rather busy. Am I out of trouble with you, Inspector Bartlett?'

'Well, we'll still need to talk to you about what's gone on but you shouldn't worry.'

'Thank you – and goodbye. Goodbye, Constable Boase.'

'You must be exhausted, Boase. Get off home for a couple of hours.'

'I am all in, I must say, sir. What about you – it's been a long night.'

'I'm all right. I'll wait for Greet – he'll be in at about seven. I'll let him know what's happened then see if I can get home myself for an hour or two. Go on. Off you go.'

Boase didn't need asking a second time. He went to the door then turned back to Bartlett.

'Sir, you didn't explain about that man – Pasty.

Why is he called Pasty Nine Lives?'

Bartlett grinned.

'He died eight times.'

'What?'

'He's had so many accidents. From a boy, apparently. At the age of eleven his boat capsized and they thought he was a goner. Then, right up until recently he's had more serious mishaps – another seven, I believe. Every time he was certain to be dead but, up he gets as if nothing has happened. Nine lives – so that makes one more left.'

'And Pasty?'

'Isn't that obvious? Now, go!'

Boase left, taking the walk back to Melvill Road. He yawned several times, feeling tired but struggling for air. The fumes from those sheds had gone for his lungs. He hadn't felt like this since the trenches. Diverting towards the sea front, Boase walked down to Gyllyngvase Beach and stood for a moment or two looking at the sea. He breathed deeply and soon his lungs felt a little clearer and his head refreshed. Walking back to his lodgings, he thought about what had happened that night. He felt bad but what choice did he have? It was him or Bull. He'd had a few lucky and narrow escapes in France and felt he'd been given another chance at life – he wasn't going to give it up now. And, what of Irene? He couldn't imagine never seeing her again. He wondered if she'd miss him. He mind went back to the friends he'd lost in France, some of them so young. How tragic that they'd never have a girl in their arms, never wake up wrapped together with the woman of their dreams. These thoughts, together with the high emotions of the night began to upset Boase and he resolved to leave them at the front garden gate as he reached the house. Entering by the kitchen door, he went upstairs and, laying across the bed, was asleep in minutes.

Bartlett left the police station at eight o'clock after a huge row with Greet. At the end of his tether and exhausted after the night's events, he had walked out. He had arranged for Sheila to be given a lift to Jim Penfold and told Greet that he would deal with her later. Having met Bert Bull, he could see how easy it was for her to have become involved with him to the point where she couldn't go back and fearing for her life. She'd had a lucky escape and no error. He reached his house and was pleased to find Irene up and about. She handed him a cup of tea and, taking one for Caroline, he went upstairs for a nap.

Sheila Parsons thanked the driver for taking her to Jim Penfold at Penryn and walked up the garden path to the front door. She knocked and waited. Jim came to the door. The two looked at each other. She was shocked to see his badly scarred face.

'Well, in you come.'

As Sheila went up the two small steps, Jim pulled her to him and hugged her.

'You silly girl. Oh, you have been bad. Why didn't you tell me how much trouble you were in?'

'Because I love you, you ol' fool.'

Jim looked at her.

'And I love you – that's why you should have told me.'

Sheila cried and attempted to dry her tears with a handkerchief.

'Come here.'

Jim took his own, folded handkerchief from his pocket and dabbed her eyes.

'That's better. Don't cry.'

'Oh! Jim. I've bin ever so foolish. An' I'm in ever such a lot of trouble.'

'Who told you that?'

'Well, Superintendent Greet – 'e says I could go to prison for a long time. I never meant no 'arm, 'onest I didn't.'

'Well, I think everyone knows that, Sheila, love. You mustn't worry. We'll sort it out.'

'Wot if we can't? Wot if I go to prison?'

Sheila was sobbing again.

'If – *if,* mind, you go to prison, well, me and Stephen and Angela will be waitin' for you when you come 'ome.'

'Do you mean it, Jim? Why would you do that? I'm such a bad person.'

'No. No you're not an' I'm not even listenin' to that sort of talk. I love you so much. I want to marry you.'

'Jim, that means so much to me. I could cope with anything just knowing that you still want me.'

'Of course I do. An' the kids love the bones of you. We'll be waitin' – whatever 'appens. Now, sit down, I'll make you some breakfast.'

Chapter Seventeen

Archie Boase had been invited to the Bartletts' house for Sunday lunch. He was nervous. Today he was going to ask to marry Irene Bartlett. Yes, she had agreed but he needed her father's permission. What if he said no? Boase felt sick as he walked up to the front door. He felt like walking quickly in the opposite direction – but then he wouldn't see Irene and he would be letting her down. This beautiful girl had agreed to be his wife, the least he could do was to make it official by asking permission. As he stood on the front step, Topper's loud bark could be heard on the other side of the door. Caroline Bartlett answered his knock.

'Hello, Archie. Come on in – we're all in the garden.'

'Thank you – how are you? Are you feeling better now? I was sorry to hear you were unwell.'

'Oh yes, I'm feeling much better now thank you, Archie. I've got some new pills and they seem to be working.'

'I'm very pleased to hear it.'

Caroline and Boase went out into the back garden where George Bartlett was sitting with Irene under an apple tree.

'Hello, Boase. Come and have a seat.'

'Hello, sir – hello, Irene.'

Irene rose from the wooden bench she had been sitting on and kissed Archie on the cheek.

'Hello, Archie. Thanks for coming.'

Irene sensed Boase's nerves and guessed what he was intending to do.

'Mum, shall we go in and lay the table? I'm sure Dad and Archie want to sit and have some beer.'

'Yes dear, all right.'

The two returned to the house.

'Got a bottle of Leonard's here for you, my boy.'

'Thanks very much, sir. Sir, there's something I must ask you.'

'What? About the Cook business? What's that then?'

Archie stood back up.

'No, sir. No, it's not about that.'

Bartlett set his beer down on the bench next to him.

'Whatever's the matter, Boase? You look so serious.'

'Well, that's because I have something serious to ask you. I'd like your permission to marry Irene.'

Bartlett took a sip of his beer and, squinting into the afternoon sun, looked up at Boase.

'Oh, you would?'

'Yes, sir. Very much.'

Boase shuffled and stared hard at Bartlett. Surely he wouldn't say no? No one else could ever love Irene as much as he did. The man's a fool to think anything else. As the younger man's thoughts ran away with him Bartlett simply said:

'OK.'

'Pardon, sir? What was that?'

'I said OK. I'm saying yes, Boase. I'd be very happy for you to take Irene on – mind, she can be

quite a handful sometimes.'
'Thank you so much, sir. Can I go and tell her?'
'Of course, go on.'
Boase didn't need to. Irene and her mother had been straining to eavesdrop from the kitchen. They hadn't heard the content but saw Boase as he came running across the lawn wearing a huge grin. He ran into the kitchen and scooped Irene up into his arms and kissed her.
'Irene, he said yes!'
Seeing Caroline looking on, he put Irene back down on the floor.
'Oh, I'm so sorry, Mrs Bartlett – it's just that, well, I'm so very happy.'
'Don't apologise, Archie – I'm happy too ... for both of you. What lovely news. Congratulations.'
Caroline Bartlett hugged Boase and then kissed her daughter.
'I'm so pleased for you, Irene – and I do so love a wedding.'
'Mum ... I'm sure that won't be for a while yet.'
All three laughed and went back into the garden where Bartlett was finishing his beer. Irene hugged him.
'Thanks, Dad.'
Bartlett looked at Boase.
'It's not all jam you know, Boase – being married. You'll never get a minute's peace. Women are always nagging. They always want you to do something – then they spend all your money...'
'George – that's not fair.'
Caroline looked indignant.
Bartlett chuckled.
'I was going on to say that I wouldn't know

what to do without my lovely wife – I think the world of her.'

'That's more like it, George. Now come on in and let's sit at the table.'

'Well, this calls for another beer I say, Boase. Join me?'

'Don't mind if I do, sir.'

Bartlett handed the bottle of Leonard's London Beer to Boase.

'Well, I would like to officially welcome you to the Bartlett family, my boy. Cheers!'

'Thank you very much, sir. I'm very happy to be becoming a part of it.'

'Well now. I don't want to put a dampener on events but did I tell you that the Cook funerals are tomorrow? Dr Cook has asked if we'd go.'

'Are we going?'

'I think we should – it's such a difficult time for them. At least we can be there to support them.'

'That's fine by me, sir.'

Bartlett kept his promise and at eleven o'clock the next morning he and Boase were at the Parish Church in Falmouth. There were a few faces they both recognised including Leon Romanov and Charlie Wentworth. Ingrid Cook was inconsolable as she watched the two coffins being brought into the church. After a short service the coffins were taken to the cemetery at Swanpool and the two Cook boys were laid to rest. Dr Cook walked over to the hedge where Bartlett and Boase were standing.

'I really appreciate you both coming – thank you. Ingrid is happy to see you here too.'

Bartlett shook the doctor's hand.

'We're so sorry that all this has happened, Dr Cook. Truly sorry.'

'Well, thank you – I know you did all you could and that that awful man has been repaid for what he has done.'

'You take care, sir. All the best now.'

Bartlett and Boase left the cemetery and walked to the police station. As they reached Western Terrace, Bartlett stopped to light his pipe.

'What a business this is. That madman must have been carrying body parts around with him – the finger, for one. And we've never found poor Desmond's head.'

'No. Probably chucked it in the sea or something, sir – in which case, we'll never find it. What do you think happened to the ring?'

'I have no idea – don't suppose there'd be much left of it now if it was in Bull's pocket. Then again, I don't suppose it matters anyway – that ring has caused so much trouble.'

'How much do you think it was worth, sir?'

'I don't know, Boase, but definitely not worth the price everyone connected with it has paid.'

'Sir, have you seen the *Falmouth Packet?* There's a big story about the Trawlerman.'

'No, I haven't seen it but no one is more pleased than me that he's been found guilty – he's led us a merry dance and no error.'

Dr Cook and his wife were bereft but had taken the time to write to George Bartlett a couple of days after the funeral with their thanks and gratitude. Sheila Parsons had been re-arrested in the light of the new evidence but was expected to be looked on kindly. She wouldn't get away with concealing the murders but her association with Bert Bull didn't mean that she had been actively involved in the deaths. She was expecting to go to prison, though, and she had accepted her fate.

'I'm going up to Bodmin tomorrow, Boase.'

'Why, sir?'

'Sheila Parsons wants to see me. I told you they're keeping her there while she's waiting for trial. Apparently she's asked desperately to see me. I was looking forward to my Sunday off but, what can I do? She specifically asked if I'd come. Greet says I can have a car – there's no chance of a train.'

'I thought that place was closed to women now.'

'It is, but they're still keeping one or two prisoners there – saves sending them to Devon I suppose.'

'Want me to come with you, sir?'

'Well, no. There's not much point in two if us hanging around. No, thanks for the offer but I'll go alone. I'm sure you've got better things to do – I don't much hold with keeping women in that place and no mistake. I've never know such depressing place as Bodmin jail.'

The car came to collect George Bartlett from his house at nine o'clock on Sunday. Greet was unaccustomed to lending cars out but Bartlett had told him it was either that or a day off midweek and that he felt duty bound to visit the woman since she requested so.

As Bartlett alighted from the car he looked up at the dark building looming in front of him. Even in the bright sunlight there was something foreboding about this place. He hurried inside and asked to see Sheila. The gaoler rummaged through a set of large keys about his waist and asked Bartlett to follow him. They wandered through a maze of corridors, Bartlett all the while listening to the chattering, moaning, shouting and crying coming from the cells. He didn't like this place, no, not one bit. Eventually they reached the cell which was holding Sheila Parsons. The gaoler fitted the key into the lock and the heavy door was pushed open. Bartlett was shocked at what greeted him. Sheila Parsons was sitting on a wooden bed under a small window. The window had thick bars and the wooden slats were bare. She sat with her knees up and her head resting on them. She looked up as the door opened.

'Hello, Sheila. I hear you wanted to see me?'

Sheila stared at him and looked as though she didn't recognise the visitor. She retreated back into the corner.

'Sheila, it's me ... George Bartlett.'

'Mr Bartlett? Oh. I'm ever so pleased to see you, ever so pleased.'

She swung her legs around to the floor and pulled the dirty hessian frock down over her knees. Bartlett looked at the gaoler.

'I think you can leave us now, thank you.'

'No.'

'What?'

'No. I can't do that. It's regulations.'

'Well, my good man, I think you'll find that you can – that is unless you want me to speak to your superior. I've have come a long way today and I'm not in the mood for your regulations – so scarper!'

The man objected no further and left, locking Bartlett and Sheila in the cell.

'Are they looking after you properly in here, Sheila?'

'Wot's properly? They won't let me 'ave a bath, me 'air's filthy and I don't feel well. It's 'orrible in 'ere – I know you think I deserve it and, well, yes I do but it's just unbearable, Mr Bartlett. Can't you get me out? I'd rather be dead.'

'No you wouldn't, Sheila. Don't talk like that. It's not at all pleasant in here but hopefully it won't be long – and I'm hoping that you'll be looked upon favourably by the court. Is there anything I can have sent in for you?'

'No. I'd love to see Jim an' the kids but they couldn't come 'ere – just look at it ... look at me.'

Sheila swept her fringe back from her face and revealed a large bruise on the side of her forehead.

'How did you get that bruise, Sheila?'

'I banged me 'ead on that shelf up there.'

'You sure?'

'Yeah.'

'I'm going to speak to my superintendent when 1 get back to Falmouth, Sheila – ask him if he can pull any strings ... maybe move you to somewhere else while you're waiting. But don't get your hopes up. I'll see if there's anything to be done. You haven't really told me why you asked to see me.'

'I dunno. S'pose to ask if you could get me out

– an' you've just said you'll try. And it's lovely to see a friendly face. Ta for comin' – really.'

'And there's nothing else?'

'No. Please try Mr Bartlett. Won't you?'

Sheila wiped a tear on her sleeve and returned to her position on the wooden bed. Bartlett patted her arm and knocked on the door to be let out. As he went back to the main area of the building he passed the office. The door was open. Bartlett knocked and stuck his head around the door. A large prison warden sat behind a desk eating a pasty.

'I've just been to see Sheila Parsons.'

'Oh, 'ave you – she's trouble, mark me.'

'Why do you say that? What has she done?'

'She's got a slack jaw and nothing to say.'

Bartlett took exception to what he considered a rather unfair observation. The warden slurped his tea, most of it dripping on to his tunic.

'Look, can't you make her a bit more comfortable – at least give her a pillow or a blanket?'

'This is a prison – not an 'otel.'

'She needs better food by the looks of it too – can't you do anything?'

'No – this is a prison.'

The warden continued with his food. Bartlett left before he became even more angry and upset. He left by the front door and returned to the waiting car.

It was five o'clock in the afternoon when George Bartlett returned to his home in Penmere. As ever, Topper was waiting to greet his master.

'Oh, what a day – I'm so pleased to see you,

Topper, really I am. Where is everyone?'

'We're in here, George. Irene's just looking at wedding dresses.'

Bartlett went into the parlour. He kissed his wife.

'Hello, princess. Everything all right?'

'Yes, dear. We're just about to have a cup of tea and some cake. Sit down.'

'Wedding dresses now, is it?'

'Not really, Dad – I just saw some pictures in this magazine – I'd never have anything as extravagant as these.'

'It's only once, dear – you should have whatever you like ... shouldn't she, George? George?'

Bartlett had slumped down in his armchair and was fast asleep.

'I'll get him some tea, Mum. He's exhausted.'

The following day, Bartlett was more than exhausted; he was feeling extremely unwell. Unaccustomed to this, he got up and dressed for work. Sitting at the breakfast table with Topper at his feet, Bartlett drank his tea.

'Would you like some toast, Dad?'

'No thanks, Irene. I don't much feel like eating.'

'Dad, you can't go out like this. You should have a day off.'

Irene was not used to seeing her father decline breakfast – in fact, it was unheard of.

'I can't have a day off, I've got too much to do.'

'Dad, you've done so many extra hours lately with this big case of yours – look at you, you're exhausted. Archie will be there – he can take care of things for one day. This case has been really stressful for you, Dad. Please stay home and rest today. You can go back tomorrow.'

'I'm beginning to feel tempted. It's just a little tiredness, that's all. You're probably right – this has all taken it out of me.'

Bartlett agreed with his daughter and had no strength to argue further. He took his tea and sat in the garden with Topper. He'd be fine tomorrow he thought to himself. He was getting old and didn't like the way old age was making him feel – still, it was better than the alternative; look at those two Cook boys, cut down in their prime. And his own dear son. Yes, he'd been given chances that his son would never have and he must make the best of it.

Bartlett spent a quiet day at home with Caroline and Irene, both of them insisting that he did nothing at all. By six o'clock, boredom having set in, he took Topper's lead down from the little peg in the hall and called for the dog. Topper came running in from the garden.

'Fancy a walk, boy? Come on then, let's put your lead on. I need to get out – a rest is all well and good but I need to get some fresh air. Would you like that?'

The dog barked approvingly and the pair left the house and took a walk across to Swanpool beach.

Feeling refreshed after his unplanned day off, Bartlett looked at the clock in his office. It was half past eight. Just as he opened the door to ask for tea, Boase appeared.

'Morning, sir. You all right today? I heard you were unwell?'

'Yes. Yes, I think so, Boase. Thank you. I was just about to ask Penhaligon for some tea – want one?'

'I wouldn't say no, sir. Oh, here's your newspaper.'

Boase placed the *Falmouth Packet* on Bartlett's desk and, pulling out his chair, sat behind his. He rummaged in his pocket and pulled out a paper bag.

Bartlett sat in his chair. He looked across at Boase and thought his assistant to be uncommonly subdued.

'What are you having there?'

'Just a piece of fruit cake, sir – want some?'

'No thanks. You wouldn't believe the number of papers Greet's given me to complete – like I've got nothing else to do. I'll just have a drink then I'll get on with it. Much happen here, yesterday?'

Boase put down the cake as Penhaligon brought in two cups of tea. Boase waited until the constable had left the room before he spoke.

'We had some bad news yesterday, sir. I didn't want to come and bother you with it yesterday and I heard you'd be back today and I wanted to tell you myself...'

'Tell me what, Boase? What's happened?'

'It's Sheila.'

'Sheila Parsons?'

'Yes. Something terrible happened. We heard first thing yesterday that she'd killed herself. I'm so sorry, sir.'

'Killed herself?'

Bartlett leaned back in his chair and looked out of the window. He couldn't take this in.

'But ... *how?* What happened?'

'She managed somehow to get hold of a razor blade and cut herself ... looks like she bled to death. They won't admit it but my guess is they left her alone all night without checking on her. They said they found her in the morning when they unlocked the cell.'

'Oh, no. This is my fault, Boase. All my fault.'

'No it isn't, sir. How could it be?'

'Well, I haven't seen you since I went up to Bodmin – she was in a terrible way. She asked me to get her out and I resolved to speak to Greet. Then yesterday I wasn't here – just at home, wasting my life away and I intended to speak to him this morning. Oh! What have I done?'

'You couldn't have known she'd do this, sir. No one could.'

'But I should have done something. She was in a very bad way.'

'What could you have done even if you'd spoken to Greet? What could he have done? Nothing! You can't ever beat the authorities on something like this.'

'But she had so much to look forward to; she was truly sorry for what she had done. She was just misguided, that's all. She was looking forward for the first time in her life – to being with Jim and settling down. Oh, my word – has anyone told him?'

'I think Greet went round there yesterday, sir. He knows now.'

'Well, I wouldn't envy him that job – Penfold thought the world of that girl. What a business. What a world.'

'Come on, drink your tea, sir, before it gets

cold. Look here's your paper, you haven't even seen it yet – you know how you like to have a little look at the gossip.'

Bartlett leafed through the *Falmouth Packet,* scanned the article about the Trawlerman, then sighed and laid the paper down on his desk.

'Oh, no. I don't believe this. Well! Oh, my. It never rains but it pours.'

'What is it, sir? What's happened?'

'Pasty Nine Lives is dead.'

'Really? How?'

'Says he was rowing across the river when he had a heart attack – looks like he fell out of the boat and drowned. What a terrible thing.'

'That's very sad, sir. But he *was* an old man.'

'Well, yes. Looks like that was the last of his nine lives then. Poor old soul.'

Bartlett closed the paper and turned his chair to face the window. He should really quit this lark while he still had some time left. He didn't want to die doing this job, while going about his duties. Yes, he liked the job – but he wasn't prepared to kill himself over it. He turned back to his desk and drank his tea. As he sat there his thoughts kept returning to the future. There was Boase and Irene now, soon to be a married couple – and children, hopefully. Yes, a new generation could be on the horizon and he, Bartlett, could start winding down safe in the knowledge that he had done his best.

The publishers hope that this book has given you enjoyable reading. Large Print Books are especially designed to be as easy to see and hold as possible. If you wish a complete list of our books please ask at your local library or write directly to:

Magna Large Print Books
Magna House, Long Preston,
Skipton, North Yorkshire.
BD23 4ND